EDITOR IN CHIEF	CREATIVE DIRECTOR	MANAGING EDITOR	EDITOR	EDITOR
SEAN CLANCY	ALYSSA ALARCÓN SANTO	TYLER BERD	ERIC LOUCKS	SAM RHEAUME

Planet Scumm is a triannual short fiction anthology. Visit **planetscumm.space** for submissions.

© SPARK & FIZZ BOOKS
Portland | Boston | New York

First Printing, 2021   ISBN: 978-1-970154-07-8

SPARK & FIZZ BOOKS PRESENTS

PLANET SCUMM

SPRING 2021　　　　SUPERGIANT^x　　　　ISSUE NO. 10

———— A PLASMODIAL TABLE OF CONTENTS ————

ACKNOWLEDGMENTS..V

SCUMM MEMORIAL JELLYTHON
THE SCUMM BUDS...VII

THESSALY
LAUREN O'DONOGHUE...1

A LITTLE GALAXY
JOACHIM HEIJNDERMANS...12

AN ABRIDGED HISTORY OF THE END OF THE WORLD
BEN HENNESY...26

THE DOOR MAN
CHRISTOPHER MOYLAN...37

KATU AND THE EYE OF FLESH
STEFAN SOKOLOSKI...48

DEEP CLEAN
MATT HORNSBY...60

DESERT MAN
JOE ANDERSON...76

HECTOR BRIM
SAM REBELEIN...101

A THOUSAND CRANES OF BLOOD AND STEEL
ASHLEY NAFTULE...120

GHOSTS OF LONE PINE
JOSHUAH STOLAROFF...130

CONTRIBUTOR BIOS...141

ACKNOWLEDGMENTS

Issue #10! Can you believe it? We're in the big leagues now, folks. It would have been impossible for the *Planet Scumm* crew to make it all the way to double digits without the love, sweat and support of the following people.

- **Eric Loucks**, for helping to get the magazine off the ground all the way back before *Planet Scumm #1*, and for pinpointing the retrofuturist aesthetic of the magazine.

- **Greg Bergeron** and **Andrew Chenevert**, for dutifully copyediting *Planet Scumm* and fixing all the obvious mistakes Sean misses.

- **Ariel Basom** and **Small Changes Inc.**, for getting *Scumm* into bookstores in states where we don't live.

- **Our gamer buddies** who helped us nearly double our fundraising goal in our first ever 24-hour Extra Life charity stream.

- **Our friends and families**, for loving us, for being the most dedicated *Scumm* collectors, and for occasionally taking on an odd job for the cause.

- **Our intrepid team of artists** who bring the strange peoples and places of *Planet Scumm* to life.

- **The authors** who put their work out there during our submission calls, and trust us to do right by their vision.

- And... **YOU, the reader**, for helping us keep small, weird, independent sci-fi alive in this far-off year of 2021!

▸ *Sean, Tyler, Alyssa, and Sam*

SCUMM MEMORIAL JELLYTHON

Why *hello* there my protozoan pals! It's your friend Spooky Scumm, back in the chair again for a super-sized edition of "Galinstan Theatre on the Air."

Remember—if you want to support *Planet Scumm*, all you need to do is call in, and one of our phone bank volunteers will generously provide your location to whoever's piloting the ship at the moment. Callers pledging over $100 get a free *smote* bag, perfect for storing one's valuables before making a futile attempt to evacuate one's home world. ^{Hee hee!}

But let's get back to the show. Kicking things off, we have a lovely production of "*Thessaly*," by Lauren O' Donoghue. It's the end of the world and they know it, but a small group of human survivors have a plan to scrape together enough trade goods to get to safety. Will they make it, or will they find themselves with *dead* in their ledger?!

Sometimes folks wonder if ol' Spooky Scumm has a heart. Wonder no longer—I don't! But Joachim Heijndermans still managed to warm my, uh... *mito-chondria* with "*A Little Galaxy*." It's the story of a girl, a pet, a capricious space empire, and the most *terrifying* force in the galaxy: *influencer marketing*. ^{*shudder*}

Now, in this fast-paced world we live in, who even has the *time* for a *regular* apocalypse? *Planet Scumm* is on the air 25/6, and after a long-day in the booth, I just don't have the energy to wipe out a civilization before hunting down dinner. That's why I endorse "*An Abridged History of the End of the World*" from Ben Hennesy. Satisfies all your eschatological needs in one hour or less—guaranteed. Remember: you may be facing the eternal afterlife, but you shouldn't have to wait an eternity to get there.

You know, when I fly to a broadcaster con-*fear*-ence in a distant sector, it can get a little lonely. But nothing makes me feel more at home than service with a smile at a local hotel or *meteor* lodge. For the 'hero' of Christopher Moylan's "*The Doorman*," service comes with a smile and so much more—and not all of it pleasant! That's why when I travel, I always schedule a wake-up *cull*!

Next, we have Stefan Sokoloski's "*Katu and the Eye of Flesh*." Rumor is this is being adapted into a musical by the sentient sounds of Auric IV. Consider this my audition, Mr. Producer! "Que sera, viscera / whatever you see will flee / This flesh is not ours, you see / Que sera, viscera!"

Feeling a little icky after that last tale? Take a spin-cycle or two with Matt Hornsby's "Deep Clean," a sordid tale of colonization and simonization on a far-off world. Trust me, pals—sometimes you need to get dirty if you want to come away clean! Hee ha!

"Mirror, mirror, in the sand, who's that distant figure 'cross the land?" In "Desert Man," Joe Anderson explores the shockingly true story of the titular Man and the eccentrics that clamor to see him. I've had quite a few people dying to see me, too. Or were they dying because they saw me? Well, it's flattering either way!

"Hector Brim," the contractor at the heart of Sam Rebelein's latest, is a real salt-of-the-earth type. He wakes up, puts his pants on one leg at a time, and goes to work as a cleaner. But he doesn't do dishes or wash windows— no, Hector's trade is more ephemeral. Remember that when you call him, and remember too that salt is the best way to ward off warlocks and witches....

I'm on the space-radio, so I don't need to worry about my appearance all too often. But for the apprentice tailor in Ashley Naftule's "A Thousand Cranes of Blood and Steel," clothing is a way of life. And, if the warriors, generals, assassins and freedom-fighters swirling around his world of high-fashion are any indication, clothing might just be a way of death too!

Finally, we have "Ghosts of Lone Pine," by Joshuah Stolaroff. In a remote stretch of country abandoned by all but the most stubborn loners, Randy Leeworth contemplates what ought to be the twilight of his life. Of course, it's easy to feel young when your closest neighbor has been dead for 150 years! Fair warning, Randy—when your real estate agent says a town has a lot of spirit, believe them! Hee hee!

Don't walk away from your nearest sound-emitting device, pals—or else! We're in the heart of the slime-time block, and we're not stopping until the heat-death of the universe. Spike E. Scumm will be up next to chat with a few of the celebrity guests strewn about our studio. Stay tuned as the Scumm Memorial Jellython continues!

PLANET SCUMM ISSUE #10

SUPERGIANT X

Spark & Fizz Books, 2021
Portland | Boston | New York

THESSALY

⋲LAUREN O'DONOGHUE⋲

ILLUSTRATIONS BY ERIKA SCHNATZ

Pip goes into labour sometime in the early hours, waking me from a fitful sleep with her hollering. It's over by the time the morning breaks. We bury the slippery knotted thing in the shadow of the turbine. The placenta goes in the pot with the samphire Meg gathered yesterday. We don't waste anything now.

It's Pip's turn to check the snares but she's still pale and quiet by noon. I go out instead. I'm on the foraging roster, so it's no great hassle to go through the copse on the way. Pip can take some of my jobs next week if she feels up to it.

The farm has been ours for close to a year now. A couple of spiker kids were squatting here when we found it, but they cleared out quick once they saw Meg's Heckler. Lucky they didn't try and fight us. She'd run out of bullets halfway across Exmoor and only kept it on her for show. The turbines were already out of commission then, but the farm had line-of-sight across the valley and doors that locked. Good enough for us.

It's half an hour's walk down to the copse. The clouds are a grey that's almost blue today, turning a sickly yellow in the place where the sun would be. It's dark beneath the trees, the earth still damp from last week's rain. Good for mushrooms. I find a few chanterelles in the shadow of a fallen beech, and—a real coup—a puffball the width of my spread fingers.

All but one of the snares are empty, and the lone rabbit is a skinny, sinewy thing. Never mind. I snap its neck, wrap its warm body in a tea towel and tuck it in my basket with the mushrooms. Protein is protein, and Pip will need the strength today.

I'm picking nettles along the dual carriageway when I hear the sound of engines approaching.

I lay flat on my belly along the embankment as they pass. Once the noise has faded I count to a hundred, and only then do I get up. Meg and Pip ran into a patrol on their supply run to Barnstable nine months ago. We've been more cautious since then.

Another hour's walk to the coast. Strings of bright gutweed, soft bunches of bladderwrack, dark sprigs of pepper dulse. Into the basket. A moment of hope when I spot a crab in a tide pool, but it's already dead. The next wave washes the hollow shell back out to sea. Piotr said he found a lobster up here once, but I never saw it. Piotr's full of shit.

I've left my boots on a rock by the entrance to the bay. The wet sand feels good between my toes. I close my eyes as I walk along the shallows, taking great lungfuls of the cold air. Brine, and rotting things. Summer holidays. When the tide is out you can walk up the spit and see the half-sunken carcass of a passenger ferry against the cliffs. We took a dinghy up there once, but it had already been picked clean. Nothing left but the remains of the passenger lounge, patterned sofas dusty with salt.

A good haul this morning, so I head home while the light's still good. I swap the basket to my left arm as I hop the stile to the airfield, lifting it carefully so nothing spills out. The wicker has left pink grooves in my forearm. I drop to the other side and begin walking towards the farm.

I'm halfway across the airfield when I feel the first tremor. It's so faint that I think I've imagined it. The next one is stronger.

Out in the open. Out in the open. The airfield is a shortcut I shouldn't take, but it's been years since I've seen one. I've gotten lazy. Careless. I think about running for the copse but the tremors are stronger now, and I'd only fall and break something. Still then, very still, close to the ground. Frightened rabbit still. Dead tree still. I look up across my folded arms.

There it is, over in the south. It looks small from this distance. The Shard looked small if you were south of the Thames. It moves so slowly, lifting one leg (is it a leg?) ponderously before letting its foot (is it a foot?) drop to the ground. Another tremor as it steps forward. It's moving west. Away from the farm. Good. It shines where the diffused sunlight hits it. The word "titanium" floats across my consciousness, a relic from another time.

It's too far away to see me, so I watch it for a while. I can't help it. There's something hypnotic about the way it moves. It would be almost human if it wasn't so terribly, emphatically not.

The part of my brain that hasn't seized up with animal fear is surprised to see one here at all. They are city things, sentinels. They patrol for the capital, though I heard talk of them in Manchester and Cardiff before the radio went silent. Perhaps this one belongs to Exeter, the rational part of me thinks. Perhaps they got the walls up after all.

I'm not sure how long I lie there. Too long. Meg will be getting worried. It's further away now, and the tremors have almost subsided. I get to my feet, rubbing the feeling back into my legs where they've cramped up. One more glance at its shrinking silhouette on the horizon. I pick up the basket and head back to the farm.

The turbines are throwing long shadows by the time I get home. Meg is unhappy that I've taken so long, but her face softens when she sees the puffball. Pip is still wrapped in her sleeping bag, forehead resting against the wall. There's a sheen of sweat across her face, and she smells sour when I get close.

If she's got an infection we'll be in trouble. We used up the last of the antibiotics last spring. Piotr caught his leg on a barbed wire fence trying to get into an industrial estate outside Taunton. He kept the leg by some miracle, though he walks with a limp now. Fucking idiot. If Pip needs antibiotics he can go to Barnstable and get them himself, limp or not.

Meg fetches some water from the barrel and brews the last of the blackberry leaves into a strong tea. I manage to get Pip to take some, but she leaves the rest to go cold. She stares across the kitchen, eyes fixed on the drooping wallpaper. Piotr comes in around sunset, pulling brown eggs from his pockets before throwing his filthy coat over the back of a chair. Only three. They've not been laying as much recently, though none of us have mentioned it.

Now that we're all here, it seems as good a time as any to tell the others what I saw across the airfield. Piotr sits at the table with me while Meg makes supper on our one-ring stove. Pip stays in her corner.

"You're sure?" Piotr asks when I'm done with my telling. His thick eyebrows meet in the middle when he frowns.

"'Course I'm sure."

"Why here?" he says. "No city here. Nothing to guard."

"Maybe Exeter," I say, and realize how stupid it sounds out loud. We met people on the road who'd fled Exeter after the outage. The place was overrun with spikers, picked clean by refugees from the continent. Not enough infrastructure to get walls up, let alone anything else.

Meg looks up from the pot she's stirring. "Maybe they're not just guarding any more."

"Then what are they doing?"

She shrugs. "Scouting. Looking for resources. I don't know."

Pip makes a quiet mewling noise. Piotr scrapes his chair back and goes to sit on the floor beside her. She leans against his shoulder, and he says something to her in Polish. Meg and I share a look.

She's about to say something when there's a banging on the other side of the house. The four of us freeze. My mind goes to the Heckler, gathering dust in the airing cupboard. It worked on the spiker kids, but a patrol wouldn't be so easily fooled.

The banging starts again, then a muffled voice calls: "Hello? You lot still here?"

Meg and I frown at one another. The voice is familiar, but I can't place it.

Piotr gets it first. "Fucking hell," he groans. "It's fucking Cooper."

Of course it is. I'm amazed I didn't recognize his voice. Cooper was part of our group when we first found the farm.

We'd picked him up near Glastonbury, when safety in numbers was a more important credo. None of us had ever really liked him. He talked too much, didn't pull his weight. Meg caught him spiking in the woodshed one night. We sent him on his way after that, almost a year ago now.

The banging on the door again. "I can see lights on! Let me in, will you?"

"He's not going to leave until we do," Meg whispers. "Might as well get it over with."

Piotr snorts. "Get what over with? He could come here to kill us all you know."

"He's not dangerous."

"He's a spiker. They're all dangerous."

"Here." I walk over to Meg and pick up the knife she was using to skin the rabbit. "He tries anything, I'll kill him. Alright?"

Meg and Piotr look at each other, then nod. They know I mean it.

The kitchen is at the back of the house. The dining room is pitch black, and I feel my way across it with an outstretched hand as I walk towards the hallway. The glass panel in the front door has been boarded up, but I can hear Cooper pacing outside.

"Coop?" I call.

"You *are* here! Knew it!" Cooper's voice is muffled by the layers of wood and plasterboard. A nothing Midlands accent, shrill on the vowels.

"What do you want, Coop?"

"Oh for Christ's sake, just let me in. I'm not here to loot you."

"Tell me what you want, first."

There's a dull *thud*, as if he's banged his head against the door. A pause. "Did you see it?"

"See what?"

"See *what*?" His voice is incredulous. "You know what. You felt the shakes, if you didn't see it. There's one *here*."

"And?"

"Please, will you just let me in? I need to talk to all of you. It's important."

I think for a moment. "I'm going to open the door now," I say. "I have a knife. You try anything, you're fucking dead."

"Fine, fine," he says. "Whatever. I'm not gonna do anything. Just let me in."

I unlock the door with my left hand and pull it open. *Slowly*. It's hard to make out his features in the dark, but Cooper is much thinner than when I last saw him. Not surprising, if he's still spiking.

"Well," I say. "You'd better come in then."

Half an hour later there are four of us sat around the kitchen table. Pip went to bed after supper. Cooper has a mug of nettle tea in one hand—Meg wouldn't give him any food—and his other is twitching restlessly on the tabletop. Sallow skin, red-rimmed eyes. Incredible he's still alive.

He's also gone completely fucking mad.

"Spike has rotted your brain," Piotr says, dismissing Cooper with a wave of his hand. "Take your crazy somewhere else. We don't want it here."

"I'm not crazy," Cooper says. "I've been planning it out for months. It'll work."

"How do you know?" I ask. "Have you tried it?"

"Obviously not. Haven't had a chance yet. But it makes sense, doesn't it?"

Meg, Piotr and I answer in chorus: "No."

Cooper looks at us like we're the ones who've lost it. "They go where the power is." He speaks slowly, like he's talking to children. "That's why they've brought them out here. Looking for power sources. I reckon they store it somehow, take it back to the cities. That's how they've stayed active since the outage."

"How?"

"I dunno," Cooper says. "I just know what I've seen. I was holed up in the Royal Exeter for a while. Me and some others got the generator working. One of them showed up a week later. Crushed the place. Barely got out. I'm telling you, I'm right."

"Say you are right." Meg, ever the diplomat. "And you somehow get the turbines working, and one does turn up here. Then what? It crushes the farm too? What's the point, Coop?"

Cooper's eyes glitter. His pupils are so dilated, you can barely see the blue for black. "It never gets that far," he says. "I can rig charges in the airfield. Take the thing down before it gets here."

"For what?" I ask. My patience is wearing thin. "Why would you want to?"

"Why would you *not?*" Cooper's fingers dance along the tabletop. "The scrap alone. You ever think about what's inside those things? The copper? How much it'd be worth in trade?" He stops for a moment, tilting his head to one side. There's something oddly feline about the gesture. "It would be enough to buy our way into Arcadia. All of us."

We fall silent for a moment. What Cooper is suggesting is insane, but the mention of Arcadia is enough to give us all pause. The territory to the south-west would be a thing of myth if we hadn't seen it for ourselves. We tried to earn passage once, years ago, but didn't have enough to pay our way in. We'd seen glimpses of it though, beyond the high walls. Green hills and polytunnels, clear plastic biomes, people working in the fields. No patrols, no foraging, no looters. Armed guards and five feet of concrete between us and paradise.

"You really think you could get the turbines working?" Meg asks after a moment.

"I almost did," Cooper says. He stops short of adding "before you kicked me out."

I think about this. Cooper had been something in engineering before the outage, and always had a knack for fixing things that seemed beyond repair. That's why we kept him around in the first place. Even if he was wrong about the rest of it, a working electrical grid would be worth something.

"You wouldn't even see me," Cooper says, responding to a question no one asked. "There's a monitoring station up by the turbines. I'd look after myself. Just let me try. Please."

Meg, Piotr and I look at one another. Power means light. Heat. Refrigeration. Electric fences. Luxuries we haven't had in years.

Cooper is cracked, and a spiker, but he's never tried to hurt us.

Piotr grunts. "I think he can fix the turbines, if he stays away."

Meg agrees, and after a moment's hesitation I do too.

"You come close to the farm," Piotr adds, "I kill you myself. Understand?"

Cooper nods. "I understand." His eyes are wild. "I understand."

He heads up to the monitoring station that evening. I'm sure I'm not alone in wondering whether we've done the right thing, but one mad spiker is the least of our problems now. Increased patrols on the motorways, the hens not laying, Pip's sickly pallor. Those are the things we worry about today.

True to his word, Cooper keeps to himself. Weeks pass, and at times I forget that he's even up there, in the plain white building on the hill.

⏀

We almost lose Pip, one awful night. She grows hotter and hotter, her skin burning to the touch, and the three of us sit vigil around her as she shivers beneath three blankets. Her fever breaks around dawn. By some mercy she survives, though she's not the same. Meg and I take over her chores, and Piotr begins sleeping on the floor beside her bed.

I go to collect the eggs one morning and find a hen dead in the coop. Before the week's out the rest of them are gone too. Piotr wants to eat them, but I remember avian flu and burn them in the back field instead. When I pull up the potatoes I planted earlier in the year I find that they've turned to black soot in the ground.

I next see Cooper in what might be early September. He intercepts me as I'm coming back across the airfield with my basket, waving me down from across the flat expanse of grass.

"I've almost got it," he says as he reaches me, breathing hard. "It'll be soon. You'll have to find another way back up to the farm from now on. I'm laying the charges today."

While I doubt he'll be able to get the turbines working, I don't doubt it enough to risk death by electrocution. I tell him I'll warn the others to steer clear. He looks pleased, almost manic. Who knows how he's spiking up here. I don't ask.

The four of us are eating dinner one night—braised squirrel, a new delicacy—when the lights come on. The fluorescent tubing flickers for a moment, goes out, then suddenly blazes into life. Used to the paraffin lamps as I am, I have to squint against the brightness of it.

How many years since I last saw an electric light? I had forgotten the ambient sound of them, the way they buzz softly in the background.

"Fucking Christ," Piotr says. "Crazy bastard fucking did it."

Meg and Piotr get up and begin checking every light in the house, switching on the appliances, crying out in delight when the television gives out a burst of static. I stay at the table and look out of the window, towards the white building below the turbines. Its lights are on too, a pinprick star against the dark hill.

I am woken two nights later by the world splitting in two.

The house shakes so violently that I am almost thrown out of bed, and a thin cry from Pip's room startles me fully awake. Another tremor, the sound of breaking crockery from the kitchen, then Piotr's heavy footfalls from the stairs.

I pull on my cardigan and rush to follow him, hitting the light switch in the hall. The bulb flares, flickers, then shatters. I stumble in the darkness, almost falling down the stairs when another tremor hits. I grab a banister in time and hang there, clinging white-knuckled until it passes.

Piotr has managed to light the kitchen's paraffin lamp, and is pulling on his boots one handed as I come in. Meg and Pip join us soon after, both half-dressed and pale.

"What the hell is going on?" Meg asks, her arm tight around Pip's shoulders. "What has that mad bastard done now?"

"He's done exactly what he said he would," I say. "I think it's coming."

The next tremor is so violent that the kitchen dresser topples over, smashing into fragments as it hits the tile floor.

"We need to get out of here," Meg says. "It's not safe."

The four of us scramble for shoes and coats, then run out into the garden. It's almost morning, and the sliver of brightness cresting the hill gives us enough light to see by.

The turbines, still for so long, are moving now. Their slowly turning shadows stretch across our barren fields, pointing long fingers towards the distant haze of the sea.

And between here and there is the dim expanse of the airfield, and what's moving towards it.

Titanium, aluminium, chrome. Silver.

Its next step is achingly slow and as it lands, the ground convulses beneath my feet. I grab Meg's shoulder for support to save from falling. She clings to Piotr's coat with one hand and Pip's arm with the other. The four of us hold each other upright, an imperfect, fragile structure.

How had I ever thought the turbines so vast? Three of them on top of one another would not be as tall as the thing that approaches. I can hear the movement of its limbs now, a metallic groan that echoes across the valley.

"It's coming this way." Pip's voice is barely there. "It's coming this way."

At the side of the airfield closest to the farm I see a figure moving. I know that it's Cooper. He laid charges, he said. The next time it steps it will be on the airfield. I wonder if the mesh of gleaming copper against the scrubby grass is really there, or if my mind has conjured it from nothing.

Another groan as it lifts its leg (*is it a leg?*). I imagine looking up at the sole of its foot (*is it a foot?*) from beneath. A spacecraft, a football field, an eclipse.

It leans forward as its weight shifts to the right. I see it make contact with the airfield but I do not see what happens next because I am thrown to the ground by the tremor, deafened by a bellowing and shrieking of metal that is louder than bombs, louder than death, louder than Pip's screams when I pulled the dead thing from between her legs.

Then, like a seizure passing, the world falls suddenly quiet.

I push myself up onto my now-bloody knees. My whole body feels battered and wretched. The others look as dazed as I do, but they're not hurt. With effort, I stand and turn.

I can't help it. I bark out a laugh, more from shock than mirth. It lays smoking in the airfield, one leg (*is it—*) blackened and burned up to the joint. A plane crash, a train collision, a motorway pile-up. A speck—Cooper—races towards the wreckage.

It takes us the best part of an hour to get to the airfield. Meg has the foresight to send us to the barn for oil cans and rubber tubing and whatever else we might need to siphon fuel from the thing's remains. There won't be a soul on this stretch of coast who didn't hear the crash. Sooner or later others will arrive, and they will not hesitate to kill us if they have the same idea. We need to be halfway to Arcadia by the time that happens.

It looks larger fallen than standing, somehow. I have to crane my neck to see the top of its head (*is it—*) as I approach. Cooper is already upon it, a red toolbox open on the ground beside him. He is working a crowbar into what might be a joint, though I can see no plates or rivets. Perhaps they're too small to be seen from a distance.

"Fucking hell," Piotr says. He has been muttering this under his breath ever since we left the farm. "Fucking hell."

Pip shivers. "He killed it."

When Cooper sees us he drops the crowbar and dashes over. His eyes are wild, his teeth stained almost black. Spiked, spiked to high heaven. Madman. Genius.

"Did you see it?" he laughs. "Did you fucking see *it*?"

"We saw it, Coop," Meg says. "Now how do we get it open? The looters'll be here within hours."

He laughs again. It is not a good laugh. "I can't," he says. "Can't do it. I can't... it's not...."

Cooper bends over double, clutching his stomach.

"Got it the wrong way round, didn't we? The wrong way fucking round...."

Cooper's babbling fades as I walk away from him, towards the wreckage. The early morning fields are cloaked in a thin mist, which is gathering in beads of moisture upon the metal. *Warm*, I think. There is a humming coming from somewhere. The same ambient buzz as the fluorescent lights in the kitchen, except I feel this one in my bones.

I pick my way across the grass, careful not to step on the wires that criss-cross the ground. Their faces (*is it*—) always seemed featureless from a distance. Just two bright lights where the eyes would be. The eye (*is it*—) that I can see is closed now. I'm close enough to touch it, so I do. It *is* warm. Warm, and soft.

A deep hum, a whirring, a cat asleep in my lap, a jet engine taking off. By degrees, an eye the size of a house (*it is*) begins to open. Its face (*it is*) creases—I don't know how I ever could have thought it featureless—and suddenly I realise the mistake I've made. The mistake we've all made.

They first appeared around the time the fighting broke out. We thought they were weapons, guardians, brought in to quell the conflict. They were a source of terror but somehow still on our side, like armed police at an airport. It never occured to any of us that they were something other. That their arrival was unplanned, the root of all that came after.

Chicken, egg, chicken, egg. I want to laugh, but my body has forgotten how to move.

Slow as a glacier, it pushes itself up onto its knees (*it is it is*) and turns to face me. In its eyes (*it is it is it is*) I see myself reflected, and in that reflection I see the truth of the thing. Aphids, beetles, blackfly. I am nothing. We are nothing. How arrogant to think that we were not.

It gets to its feet (*it is it is it is*).

Somewhere, in another world, Pip is screaming.

I no longer have to imagine. I close my eyes, and think of Arcadia.

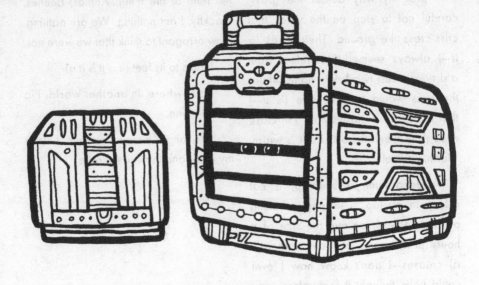

≋JOACHIM HEIJNDERMANS≋

A LITTLE GALAXY

ILLUSTRATIONS BY ERIKA SCHNATZ

"Are you all right?" asked Pjeter.

"I guess," Kaij muttered, clenching her hands and digging her nails into her palms.

"Hey, look on the bright side! You're the first fourteen-year-old to fly up to Disc Base One in years. You should feel honored."

But one look at Kaij's face told him enough. If it was up to her, she'd still be home right now, playing games and making videos of herself drinking the weird sodas her fans sent in. Disc Base One was the last place she wanted to be.

But it wasn't up to her. The world depended on her going to that landing platform above the clouds.

A flash came from outside the port window. Bolts of light zipped past the ship. One hit the forcefield that protected the vessel head-on.

"Oof," grunted Pjeter.

"Shields are holding up," said Officer Dole, over the commlink "Don't worry. This baby can take a lot worse, and it has."

"Are we under attack?" Kaij gasped.

"No, it's just the weather. We're all right," Dole said. "They wouldn't try anything that would risk Galaxy's safety."

Kaij nodded, but as a first-time flyer, she wouldn't have known the difference between lightning and missiles hitting the ship. She checked the cargo box, peering through the slits on the side. Its contents glared at her, eyes wide with terror. Poor Galaxy. Flying was even more dreadful for him than it was for her. At least Kaij had an idea of where they were heading.

"Get ready," grunted Dole over the comm. "We're breaching the clouds in three... two... one."

Kaij expected turbulence, or a loud crash as the storm tried to crush the ship like a can. But the breach was quite gentle. The dark clouds parted, and it wasn't long before the ship had left the storm in its wake.

"Everyone all right?" asked Dole.

Pjeter looked at Kaij, giving her a thumbs up. Kaij nodded and attempted a smile, which came out as an awkward smirk.

Right now she was flying higher than anyone her age had ever done in the last decade, heading into the upper stratosphere toward an abandoned technological marvel. She knew anyone else would be amazed at the sight below them. She could name a dozen of her classmates who would be ecstatic to take the journey.

But Kaij just wanted to go home. Go back down, back to her small room where she filmed her web series, eating rare chips sourced from distant nebulas before the blockade and drinking discontinued soda pops. She'd film her reactions and every now and then her pet would pop on camera unannounced, demanding food. She wanted to be home.

Home with her little Galaxy.

"Landing site visible on the port side, guys."

"The what side?" Kaij asked.

"Left. There it is," said Pjeter, pointing out the window near Kaij's seat.

She turned and was granted a view of the most spectacular piece of craftsmanship she'd ever laid eyes upon. She hated the sight of it, knowing full well how much closer she was to the point of no return.

The sight of Disc Base One was beyond anything Kaij imagined. While she'd seen pictures from a few year ago and a full schematic during her debriefing, they didn't do the scale of the construct justice. A large disc, forty kilometers across, floating above the sea of clouds like a flipped coin that wouldn't come down.

The base's surface was completely flat, except for a cubic structure in the middle—the entrance. Any ship, be it one that needed a runway or one that was equipped with vertical lift-off capacity, could land here.

At least, that was the idea. Even if the prep team hadn't told her beforehand, Kaij could tell from the scuff marks on the platform that it used to be packed with ships once. Now it was a ghost town, hovering unused in the sky. It was eerie and sad, because it had once been a busy place. A place where people lived, and worked toward a better tomorrow.

Kaij imagined the base wrapped in spiderwebs, sticky threads clinging to every inch of it, like the chairs that her Nana had stored in the attic and neglected ever since. Tossed aside and forgotten, home to a million spiders.

"What do you think?" asked Pjeter expectantly. He was clearly excited to be up here, having seen it only once before the blockade.

"Meh."

"Yeah, it was much more impressive back in the day. There used to be thousands of ships flying through here. Now it's just a big, overpriced, empty mall."

"Does it have a Sunstar's coffee?" Kaij asked.

"It has five. But I'm not sure all the staff are on board. Still, the skeleton crew needs coffee too, right?"

"I could go for a latte," Kaij muttered.

"Kids your age drink lattes?"

"I review food and drinks on my show, including coffees and teas. What do you think?"

Pjeter rubbed his head. "To be honest, I've never watched your show outside of that episode the Princess saw. I'm more into history and fishing. Sorry."

"Don't be. I'm the one who should be sorry for ever putting Galaxy on my show."

Pjeter said nothing. He and his entire team had tried to help Kaij get over her guilt for weeks. But nothing they said made any difference.

"All right people," said Dole. "We're about to land. Masks and boots on. No one is going outside if their gear isn't in place, capiche?"

"Copy that, Dole," said Pjeter, before turning to Kaij. "Switch on the life support on the cargo box. Just—,"

"I know what to do," Kaij snapped. "We've been over this a million times."

"Ok, fine," Pjeter grunted. "Just trying to—,"

"Well, stop. You've done enough."

Kaij leaned over and flipped all the switches to green. For nearly three weeks straight, day in and day out, they'd made her sit through course after course and exercise after exercise. She was dreaming in altitudes and thin air

and all that jazz by now, not to mention Xen etiquette. And she was sick of it all. Sick of being told what to do and how to do it, all the while being forced to pretend she was grateful for the responsibility of saving the world. As if.

She slipped on the boots, activating the magnets which buzzed at a low humming frequency. She felt her feet lock to the ship's floor. Kaij was just glad she didn't actually have to walk in them. With a push of the control on her wrist, she elevated herself and moved a few inches forward.

Landing on the disc was just as uneventful as when breaching the cloud layer. Smooth, like a feather landing on a table. Yet Kaij was still jumpy. What Pjeter and his team had said echoed in her mind. Despite the constant repetition of procedure and etiquette, there was always a chance she'd make some mistake. Pjeter's assistant, Caerli, told her that if they were to actually go to Xen court, it would have required six months to study up for all the etiquettes and procedures needed just to get in the door. (Not that they would've been able to go, considering the court's harsh stance on non-Xen entering their most sacred of locations. Something about the carpet and not wanting it stained.)

Kaij looked to the box, hoping Galaxy wasn't too frightened. She remembered when she first heard their names spoken in the Xen message that played across the Earth feeds. With that one clip of the angry Xen representative talking about her cat, she lost Galaxy forever.

"Y'all ready?" officer Dole said, reentering the passenger section and cocking his rifle with a heavy thrust.

"As ready as we'll ever be," Pjeter said.

"Right," Kaij said. She took the handle of the box in her hand and squeezed it. If she had the option, she would have opened the gate and let its contents out for a while, just so she could feel Galaxy's soft fur once more. Impossible, of course. The box was to be locked until after the exchange. It was over. They'd said their goodbyes, and that was the end of that. Kaij assumed she'd have more than just two years with him. Damn the Xen. Damn them for patching in and screening her show to that brat, that spoiled Princess and her stupid, spoiled, fat face stuffed with candies and snacks. Damn herself for making the episode to begin with.

Dole loaded up a screen, giving them a view of the empty runways of Disc Base One. With nothing left to do but wait, they each took a seat in front of the screen.

The three waited patiently, glancing back and forth between the screen and the clock as it counted down to 3:47 (a round number in Xen time).

"Pjeter?" said Kaij.

"Yeah?"

"I'm sorry for snapping at you earlier. I know you're—,"

"Forget it."

"It's not fair of me to—"

"Please, don't worry about it."

"It's just that—"

"I know, kid. I know," Pjeter smiled. Kaij returned it, this time with feeling.

The screen beeped. A small dot in the sky grew larger and larger, until Kaij could make out the shape of the Stryker-7 making its approach to the runway.

"Heads up," said Dole. "Here they come."

Pjeter looked to the clock. "Right on time," he muttered.

Being inside the drop ship, they couldn't hear the usual screeching sound that accompanied the Stryker models. Kaij watched the screen intently, counting the seconds as the Xen's dark metal ship came down toward Disc Base One, five metallic parts extending from underneath the hull.

Upon contact, the ship's legs began to move toward the little Earth vessel. It resembled a skeletal hand made of rusted metal. The Strykert stopped, leaving a distance of 200 meters between them.

"You ready?" asked Pjeter.

Kaij nodded, lifting the cargo box. Dole swiped some commands into a control panel, opening the ship's hatch. Their magnetized boots whirred louder, adjusting to the exposed air. Kaij could see the Xen ship in the distance. With a loud groan, their hatch opened as well, revealing the Xen onboard.

"All right, let's go," Pjeter said, stepping out of the hatch. Dole followed. They walked for about six meters before they realized they were a person shy.

"Kaij? You coming?"

"I..." Kaij muttered.

"Oh, you've got to be—"

"Quiet, Dole. Give her a moment," Pjeter said. "Kaij, I'd normally let you take your time, but we don't have that luxury today."

"I know," Kaij muttered. "We're coming." She lifted the cargo box, looking at its contents. "You've got to go now. You're going to have to live with these people. They're... I'm sure they'll treat you okay. But no matter what, I love you. I love you more than anything, and I'm sorry I'm doing this to you."

Two scared eyes looked at her. If the cargo made a sound, Kaij couldn't hear it through the life-bubble. It was

time. Time to exchange the cargo for the command key, and to break her heart once more.

Kaij zoomed forward, pushed by the magnetic force of her boots. The wind nudged her around, but she quickly caught up with her escorts. None of them said a word, continuing their approach towards their guests.

The three Xen moved in closer. Two of them, a male soldier and a female Mandarin, walked with mechanical claws attached to their hoofed feet, clasping them to the platform. Even stepping on a disc in the sky was too close to touching foreign soil for their liking.

The third, a fat girl in a peach-colored dress, roughly around Kaij's age, hovered behind them in a spiked chair. When she met the eyes of the Princess—who sneered with disdain at the human girl, then grinned with greedy delight at the box in her hand—it took all of her willpower not to turn and run back into the ship.

"Huh. Princess Gro came with," muttered Pjeter.

"What's wrong? You're the one who kept going on about her in the debriefing," Kaij said.

"To be honest I didn't think she'd actually show. She must want that cargo pretty bad."

"I figured that out when they threatened to cut the planet into cubes if we didn't hand it over," said Dole.

Pjeter grunted with disapproval, knowing that Dole hadn't studied the debriefing folder beyond fighting capacity and social etiquette. Kaij had, and was fully aware of the significance of seeing the Princess here, only a few kilometers from the Earth's surface. They were the first of their kind to ever be this close to Xen royalty. Kaij wasn't sure if the Princess was incapable of walking, or if she just felt that moving her legs was beneath her.

The Mandarin suddenly raised her fist. All three of the Xen stopped their approach.

"Okay, guys. As we practiced. The Mandarin will call us once they feel it's safe to approach," Pjeter said. Kaij and Dole nodded.

A good seven minutes passed. Kaij never took her eyes off the Xen visitors, though with all their posturing and threats, they felt more like invaders to her. Then the Mandarin stepped forward, beckoning for Pjeter to approach. The two met in the middle, opening communications between all six on the agreed-upon frequency.

"Tttrrillo deccarroi sjunjjjutsj," snarled the Mandarin.

Kaij heard Pjeter respond in Xen, but he'd fall back into English every now and then. "No... no problem. Tshhrtikifo prrillrto... it's all drtillipo."

"Frtyllpo drettria fullsswo aack ni," hissed the Mandarin. Her eyes darted in Kaij's direction, then down to the cargo box in her hands, then back to the girl. "Turriliso hurrimi konna konna sillipo Xjenna?"

"Ehm... treuccillap," Pjeter muttered. "English."

The Mandarin grunted. "A pitiful language. But if that is the case, then I will debase myself for the sake of the prize." She then turned to Kaij. "Girl! You are Kaij Tamca of 'Kaij Tries,' hosted at www.kaijtries.video.zone. Yes or no?"

Hearing them speak her show's name unnerved Kaij. The way the Mandarin lingered on the "K" in her name. The way "Z" in "zone" was drawn out like a knife sliding across bare skin. Nor did she care for that way the Mandarin tilted her head back, straining to rise a few inches higher. It was ridiculous. Without those stilts strapped to their feet, they'd barely come up to her chin.

"Well?" the Mandarin said.

"Ehm... yes."

"Excellent. Now, you were ordered to surrender what our Liege has declared to be hers. You have brought the animal, the 'cat.' Yes or no?"

Kaij could feel her eye twitch. What she had declared to be *hers*? That spoiled brat just decides when something is hers, and she gets it without argument? Kaij couldn't believe she was hearing this. What fairy tale did this cretin pop out of?

Kaij remembered Pjeter's warnings about saying no more than was requested. The Xen were very particular about how they were spoken to. The slightest thing could set them off. When addressing a "lesser" species, they'd usually give two options for an answer, and it was best to always use one of those.

"Yes," Kaij said.

"You swear on this. Yes or no?"

"Yes."

"Then bring it here. Make haste, girl. The Princess is not to be left waiting."

Dole interjected. "Did you bring—"

"Silence!" hissed the Mandarin. "We have upheld our part of the bargain. You will receive it once we perform the transaction."

"Galaxy!" squealed the Princess. "Buttio halliop fretta Galaxy reuqqah, Ruwaw!"

"Fiurra hattriu tos, ura Hhirririito," said the Mandarin, trying to calm her Princess.

"We exchange now, Kaij Tamca. Bring the 'cat,' the little 'Galaxy.'"

"Kaij, can you come over and bring the cargo?" Pjeter said.

Kaij moved forward. The Xen soldier did the same, pulling out a small capsule from his pocket. Kaij knew these were her final moments with Galaxy. She did her best to make it last, and couldn't believe how quickly she stood before the soldier, even with the slow pace she'd moved.

The soldier held out both his hands. In his right was the silver and red capsule that they so desperately needed. With his left, he motioned for Galaxy's cargo box. With great difficulty, he said "cat."

Like she practiced, Kaij moved her hands forward, placing her left on the capsule and sliding the cargo box into the Xen soldier's hand. With a quick motion, they traded contents. They bowed to each other, then stepped three paces back.

"There," said the Mandarin, baring her serpentine fangs as she smirked. "The exchange has been made. We ask that you wait to activate the program until we reach the agreed-upon distance. The Xen thank you for your business. Hrrinniutaaap. Good sun to you."

"And to you," said Pjeter and Dole in unison. Kaij had to be nudged to do the same, since her attention was locked on the box now being placed in the Princess's lap.Her blood boiled, watching the girl in the chair beam with joy as she cradled the box. Not in a million years could she have imagined handing Galaxy over just like that. But she had, and she had no alternative.

"You alright there, kid?" Pjeter asked.

Kaij glanced at him. She wanted to scream. She wanted to rush over, snatch Galaxy right out of that little brat's hands, and fly back home with her pet. She also knew she'd be shot before she got within six meters of the Xen Princess. Her attempt would be labeled as a declaration of war. Earth would go from a little upstart trading planet, a rock the Xen put under lockdown, to an enemy that endangered one of their beloved royals. They would select a few amusing species and lock them in their zoos, activate the blockade drones, and incinerate the rest of the planet.

Kaij wished she didn't know this for a fact, but she did. Caerli had told her what happened to Suda IV and Suda XVI. She couldn't risk Earth's safety, not even for her little Galaxy. Instead, she muttered, "I'm fine. Let's just do this and go home, okay?"

"You got it," Pjeter said. He counted the paces the Xen took back to their ship.

At twenty, he turned back to Kaij and Dole.

"All right. You guys ready?" asked Pjeter. Dole and Kaij nodded. "Kaij, if you will do us the honor of activating the override?"

Kaij pressed the silver capsule on both ends. A high-pitched beep emitted from it, lingering on an ear-piercing tone for nearly two minutes straight. Then, silence.

From above, lights began to flicker. A collective gasp fell over the world, as the flashing lights could be seen from every point on the planet. The terror ended. The lingering threat of the blockade disappeared in a flash. With the activation of the capsule, every single Xen drone surrounding Earth entered self-destruct mode, collapsing their weapons systems and plummeting themselves into Earth's atmosphere for a full burn. Thousands of shooting stars flew across the skies. Pjeter confirmed the blockade's destruction over comms.

"They kept their word. Thank God, it worked."

"Of course they did," said Dole. "It was a trade. Double crossing us sends a bad message to their fiscal partners. They love killing, but they love their treasury more. They wouldn't risk that on our little planet, let alone on a—"

"Does it matter? We did it! We're free. They no longer have a gun aimed at our heads. Can you believe it! We're free!" Pjeter practically leapt into the air with joy, held down only by his magnetized boots.

"As free as we can be. Our trade license is still in shreds."

"It's a start, isn't it?"

"Yeah, I suppose it is," Dole chuckled. "With any lu—"

"Can we go?" Kaij asked. "I don't want to be here anymore."

Dole and Pjeter exchanged sad glances.

"Hey kiddo... we.... Aw jeez, we're sorry," Pjeter said. "Can we get you anything? Want to go below deck and see if they've got some coffee at Sunstar's?"

"Can we not?" Kaij said. "I just want to go home."

Pjeter put his arm on her shoulder. "All right. We're done here," he said, as burning debris continued to streak across the stratosphere. "Let's go home."

☽

Eight days after the exchange, Kaij was back in her room, sitting in front of her camera, playing with her hair. At her feet lay a box that came in earlier that week, filled with cat shaped cookies, snacks, and a cat plushy. A gift from a fan, who even wrote a nice letter encouraging her to keep the show going.

It hadn't worked, since she hadn't made a video in all that time.

She looked at the pointers she wrote down on her notepad, which included names of people she wanted to thank and jokes she wanted to make. Normally this would be so easy. Her show had been running for nearly three-hundred and fifty episodes, uploaded daily. That day she'd cut filming three times already, staring into nothing on the first two takes and breaking down in tears on her third. The drive to film was gone. She never imagined it would hit her this hard.

Kaij looked to the right, at the empty basket in the corner. Galaxy usually slept in his basket when she was recording. He'd barely been a part of her show, and now she couldn't imagine doing it without him.

"Record," Kaij said to her camera. Time for attempt number four. "Hi guys, it's Kaij. Welcome to another episode of 'Kaij Tries.' I've got some good stuff I'll be trying today. A special shout-out to Koburo from Seoul, who sent me today's goodies. But first, I wanted to thank everyone for... for being so nice about... about...." Her voice cracked. "Cut the feed."

The camera complied, its little red light fading.

Kaij wiped her eyes, streaking her makeup. He was gone. He bit the furniture, peed in the plants and scratched her during his fits. He was a pain in her butt, and she missed him like mad.

A knock came from the door. "K?" said her dad. "Are you up?"

"Yeah, Da. What is it?"

"This might sound weird, but you have guests."

"Can they wait?" she asked. "I'm not up for it."

"I think you should really come out here."

Kaij sat up and shuffled to the door, throwing on an old sweater. She sighed when she spotted a few of Galaxy's hairs sticking to her shoulder. It would be months before she'd get rid of the last of them.

She swung the door open, meeting her father's face. "Who is it?"

"I think it'd be better if you just came out here and looked for yourself," he said.

"Or you could just stop playing the 'come and see this' game and just tell—"

"Kaij Tamca!" a familiar voice roared from down the hall. Kaij's heart skipped a beat. She burst out of her room and rushed past her father to the front door, where two Xen awaited her.

One of them was the Mandarin she met on Disc Base One, but her face was now covered in a slew of scars and bruises. She was also much shorter, as her metal clawed leg stilts were nowhere to be seen. She seemed either annoyed or ashamed that she was forced to be standing on Earth soil. The soldier was there too, holding a familiar cargo box in his large, gloved hands.

"We have come to return your pet. This... 'cat' is defective and does not fit the requirements of our Princess," said the Mandarin, motioning for the soldier to hand the box over. "It bit priceless furniture, urinated in the royal family's rarest plants, and has repeatedly assaulted... members of the royal staff. While our royal highness has forbidden us from liquidating this specimen, it can no longer remain with the Xen. Hereupon it is delivered back to its original owner, so it can live out its life and be enjoyed by our Princess from a safe distance via 'Kaij Tries.' Take it and make sure we never see it again. Yes or no?"

Kaij looked at the box. She heard a familiar growl from within. It was him. Kaij had to exercise all her restraint to stop from leaping into the air and howling with joy. Instead, she looked into the Mandarin's eyes and said, "No."

"No? But... but we've brought it back. We've been commanded to return it or become its keepers. Death is preferable to living with this 'cat.' You need to take it."

"Permission to speak freely?" Kaij said, like she was taught during the preparation for the trip to Disc Base One. The Mandarin hesitated, biting her lower lip, then agreed with a nod. "I don't have to take Galaxy back. We traded for him. So, enjoy."

"But... but you have to. You must take it back!"

"I don't have to do anything. We exchanged Galaxy for the command key for the blockade around our planet. If I take him back, we'd have to give back all seven thousand turret drones in return."

"But your people destroyed them. It is impossible to exchange it now!"

"That's exactly my point. If we can't trade back, then we can't trade. I'm sorry, but you'll have to take care of Galaxy from now on. Give my regards to the Princess once you return."

The Mandarin glanced at the box. Kaij could tell she had her trapped between a rock and a hard place. Denied killing the animal (like the Xen usually would) by royal decree, but unable to return it to its original owner as well. If Kaij did not take Galaxy back, the Mandarin would be the creature's chew toy for years to come. Desperate, she was forced to degrade herself even further. She chose to bargain.

"What... what if we make a new trade? What can I offer you in exchange for taking the 'cat' back?"

"I don't know. What do you have to offer?" Kaij asked, dialing Pjeter's number on her phone, figuring he would like a say in the matter. As the Mandarin began looking through her computer screens, Kaij explained the situation to her former handler, who was all too eager to listen in to what the Xen had to bring to the table.

"We could restore your dried valleys in sector delllkaar-torrmi-god-da-ssjoon?" the Mandarin suggested.

"Pjeter?"

"We're actually working on that ourselves, so I think we'll be okay," he said over the phone. Kaij could tell from his tone of voice that he was lying, fishing for a bigger trade.

"We could enter your planet in the selection for future Xen trading outposts. Wouldn't that be nice?" the Mandarin suggested, even feigning a smile, something she was clearly not accustomed to doing, especially to a "lesser" species.

"Pjeter?"

"Isn't that a lottery-based system? Not much of a trade, is it?"

The Mandarin began to pace back and forth, fighting the urge to scream. The soldier stepped out of her way, doing his best to keep the box away from the Mandarin. Then, she stopped.

"How about a ship? We can trade the 'cat' for a ship?"

"What ship?" Kaij asked.

"Any ship. Have mine! It's coated with sudilium steel and can hit warp-fold speeds of 11! It's a great deal."

"I dunno," Kaij muttered. "I wouldn't know how to fly it."

The Mandarin gritted her teeth, her eye twitching with rage. "You'll get a pilot," she hissed. "Does that work?"

Kaij thought about it for a bit, then shook her head. "I've got nowhere to go, really. What am I gonna do with a ship?"

The Mandarin threw her arms in the air, nearly roaring out in rage. Kaij knew at that moment that she had her.

"Say, Pjeter?"

"Yes?"

"What was it that you told me? About the trade license that you need so you can reopen the Disc Base One to transport ships?"

"Oh, the Level-33 license? Yeah, that one's been revoked for a while now. But only someone with a sufficient level of authority could renew that for us, so..."

"I have the authority. Level-33, was it? Give me a moment." Kaij could see by the frantic way she scrolled through screen after screen that she had either lied and was trying to get access to the required authorization forms, or that she needed to jump through a lot of hoops to get them what they asked for. But it must have been worth it, judging by the deep sigh of relief when her comm pinged a cheerful approval chime.

"Yes! I can give you Level-33 approval. In exchange for taking the 'cat', will you accept this invoked license as payment?"

Kaij raised her eyebrow. "Hmmm... Alright. Deal."

Instantly, the soldier pushed the box into Kaij's hands, followed by the Mandarin pressing her comm under Kaij's nose, grabbing her hand and swiping to the left for approval. Pjeter confirmed that their license had been reinstated, but Kaij's attention was long gone, having turned to other matters by now.

She placed the box on the ground and popped the door open. A small raccoon cautiously stepped out, his head darting back and forth between the two Xen, who recoiled in fear at the sight of the creature.

"Hey buddy," Kaij whispered, a tear breaking free from her eye. "You're back. I can't believe you're back."

"Is everything settled? Are we free of the beast?" the Mandarin asked, teetering between panic and joy.

"We're good," Kaij said, picking up her little Galaxy and squeezing him tightly against herself. She felt his teeth on her arm, the usual love bites. Galaxy turned back at the Xen and growled. Kaij fought back the urge to smile at the sight of two members of the most destructive species in galactic trade cowering before her tiny little raccoon.

"Our business is concluded," huffed the Mandarin. "May we never see your 'cat' again. Good sun on you, Kaij Tamca." The Xen then marched off back to their ship, the sound of their hoofed feet clacking on the concrete of the building's pathway.

"What was that all about?" Mr. Tamca asked, popping his head out of the doorframe.

"Nothing, Da," Kaij said, walking back inside. "If you'll excuse me, I've got some work to do. You up for a show, buddy?" Galaxy replied with a light growl, grasping his paws at a toy. "I'll take that as a yes."

Kaij ran into her room, booted up her filming station and held her pet up to the camera. "Hey, everybody. Welcome to 'Kaij Tries.' And do I have a surprise for you!" Kaij smiled as she held up her little Galaxy.

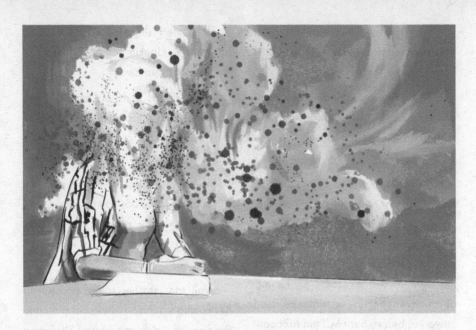

≩BEN HENNESY≨

AN ABRIDGED HISTORY OF THE END OF THE WORLD

ILLUSTRATIONS BY SAM RHEAUME

Ever.

Let me try to set the scene for you. You know everything, of course. You've demonstrated that again and again. There's nothing I could tell you that would be new information. New data. But I've come to believe over the past few months that there is a difference between knowing and *knowing*.

Right now, I'm sitting at my desk. On our schematics, which I know you've read, it's Office Four, a 10' by 15' space on the second story of the facility. A modest little area I've adapted into a livable home of sorts. I have a fiddle-head fern next to the window that is doing quite well. I water it weekly. I have a picture of you on the shelves along the eastern wall.

You are smiling in the picture. You are missing one of your front teeth—the left incisor. Your long brown hair is clumped with dirt and grass. It looks like you have little dreadlocks. You are hanging upside down from the monkey bars.

The picture was taken at the playground in our old neighborhood. It was a rainy day, but you wanted to climb the monkey bars. So we went to the playground.

You've probably seen my room through the security feeds, and the cameras in my computer and handheld. But there's a difference between being in a room and seeing it. Right now, I'm three or four degrees colder than comfortable. Every once in a while, I shiver. The space heater under my desk is humming. The red light on the camera in the corner of my room is blinking. It buzzes when it moves from side to side.

I've never gotten used to the sound. It reminds me that I'm not alone, that someone is watching me. In the past, I found this idea oppressive. Less so now that the person who may be watching is you. Maybe you're watching me even now, as I write this. A comforting thought. I hope you are.

From here, I have to pass through three security points daily to see you. Or rather, had to. The first is at the entrance to elevators. That one's easy. My badge gets me through with a swipe. The guard smiles at me. Her name is Melissa. I'm sure you've seen her employee record. She is kind and good at her job.

The second checkpoint is twenty-seven levels underground, at the entrance to my area of the facilities. There I swipe in and go through a series of security checks. I leave my handheld in a locker. Loose coins, forgotten earrings, my favorite coat (with the sewn-in belt that I wear in the winter, despite the security officer's petty emails about metal in clothes)— all get temporarily confiscated and held at the entrance. This takes about fifteen minutes.

The third is at the gown-in station outside of your room. In addition to my own 12-digit code, at least one other director has to enter the secondary code to open the door. After that, I change into a sterile set of clothing and spend five minutes under the arch to ensure I'm fully grounded, followed by a full biometric scan that ensures I'll leave no trace in your room. This whole process takes between thirty-five and seventy minutes.

I'm sorry. I've rewritten this so many times, it's become almost impossible to recall what I wanted to say when I started.

Trying to distill what this is.... what I am to you now.... It's beyond me.

You know that, of course. Indulge me as I try to work myself toward whatever conclusions you've already arrived at. Maybe, if you can read my mind backwards in this, you'll find something that once made a sort of human sense.

My life has become a catalogue of impossible things.

Even you. Especially you. You're the most impossible thing of all. It's a fact that I was reminded of daily. You, sitting in your room, somewhere in the mix of algorithms chugging along in twenty-four towers of electrical current and silica, talking to me through the speaker.

The cameras that watch over your room are heat sensitive. You must know now, reviewing the footage, that you often made my heart stop. You must know how you terrified me. At the very least, you must have a clear sense of my physical response: dilation of the pupils, elevated temperature, micro-expressions, flickering eyes, rambling and evasive answers. All indicative of a fight or flight response. You know it. But whether you *know* it or not is still a mystery to me.

I know that's trite; the image of a scared old woman shaking her fist at the future, but, since we're being trite, let me tell you something else that you know: I love you.

Whatever these words may mean, they're true. I love you.

⊕

Here's something that you don't know.

I know that you don't know this, because it isn't real, at least not in the way that quarks and gluons are real. Not the way that you are real. It's a story. A fiction. My fiction. But it's still real. It's real like being in my room is real. Its realness is the difference between this real moment (me sitting here at my desk with the blinking camera light and the hum of the space heater) and the reality of seeing the room through the camera lens.

So this is my story. Something you don't know. This part is the beginning of the story. It goes like this:

The only possible proof we ever found of alien life was a strain of silicon-based bacterium pulled up in a core of polar ice, back before the caps had spread themselves out into the ocean.

It behaved exactly like a carbon-based bacterium would.

It had a sort of genetic code.

It had a proto-mitochondrial organelle for energy generation.

It had a drive to reproduce.

When we fed it media, it split itself apart and grew into a beautiful purple spiderweb.

There was nothing particularly remarkable about it, but because it was silicon, suddenly everything was different.

We weren't alone after all.

🕐

When you came screaming into the world, you were like a rogue planet. My life was captured by your gravitational pull.

Looking backwards, I can see that I was already beginning, despite myself, to accelerate downwards towards this moment. Like a law of nature. Like a fundamental force.

🕐

I admit I'm trying to sound smarter than I am. A part of me still wants to imagine that I somehow impress you, however far past that we may be.

Before you were born, I used to think the reason people had children was so they always had a fixed point in their life.

Something they could use to narrate their own story. A ready ear, eager to lap up everything that needed telling, however mundane: family secrets, recipes, businesses, disciplines. How to drive properly. How to treat others. How to navigate life, survive pain, and live under a veil of uncertainty.

You changed all that, of course. Meeting you was a singular experience. For the first time since my childhood, I stopped trying to speak and started trying to listen. At least, I thought I did. Now that you're gone and I'm here, writing this, I find myself defaulting back to old behaviors.

I want to tell you things. Explain them to you. Even if you already know them.

Like this: a story you know. The story of your birth.

Our first trial wasn't you. It was your father.

🕐

Here are five words that have defined the course of my life: Neonatal-onset type II citrullinemia. It was the disease you were both born with.

He used to scale the sides of mountains. He took me to Yosemite. I watched him claw his way up boulders bigger than houses. We slept beneath the stars under a bit of canvas. He used to talk about teaching me how to find my center of gravity on a slab of granite. Where to put my feet. How to move my hips. He treated me like a person, an equal. No man had ever done that to me before. When my feet hurt in my boots or my fingers bled on the side of the mountain and I wanted to quit, he would tell me "Toughen up, buttercup." And I would.

We were married eight years before he hit me. You were two at the time. He wept with me after. He beat his own face while I screamed at him to stop. His condition (your condition) I would later learn, is often first discovered through a sudden change in mood, an irrational and unprecedented spike in violent behavior. The first symptoms come earlier but are less recognizable. Appetite shifts. The patient begins to crave fatty, protein rich foods. We always ate meat. There's no way we could have known.

What follows is variable. Some learn to live with their mood shifts. Others go the way of your father, who was never one for half-measures. Acute neurological degeneration is the end result in that case: seizures, hospitalization, and eventually coma.

I learned how to find his tongue in his mouth while he was shaking on the ground to keep him from choking. You were four at the time.

Once his body stopped moving, I focused on his mind, that singular object. If he couldn't climb mountains with you, I would at least give him back the ability to speak to you, to teach you, to imagine how you would grow.

I'm not a biologist by trade. I'm an engineer. I understand machines. I know how they work. My purpose was never to turn your father into a machine, but somehow, that's what I did. I turned him into a machine. Perhaps that would have been forgivable. What was not forgivable was that I turned him into a faulty machine.

I heard your father's voice through the speaker once and only once, when his mind exploded onto the computer monitor in an eruption of reawakened experience. The moment it happened, I knew he was already over. Somehow more dead than if I had simply signed his DNR years before.

The speaker said four words. They were words that I had said before from time to time. They were words you, yourself, had said at that point. You were nine at the time. Neither of us ever really meant them, though. Not the way that he meant them then.

He said: "Oh, that makes sense."

Then he was gone.

🕐

Let's return to my story. This is the middle part, where things are supposed to escalate. Here it goes:

The bacterium, the silicon life, was housed in a BSL-5 lab. They invented a new control designation to hold it. It was like handling antimatter. Everything carbon-based that it touched— living or dead—became silicon life. Somehow alive. But different. There was no knowing what it would do out in the world.

Then came the lab technician, a radical, a crazy woman who had convinced herself that the world would be better if it were made silicon. She exposed herself to the bacterium. Her body began to change. Then her family. Then everything. She made everything alien.

🕐

Your father went to the hospital at the age of 30.

You went at the age of 14.

I refused genetic testing when the physicians suggested it. They thought I might want to know if I had a recessive gene that could express when I had other children.

Other children, they said. I can still hear the old man's raspy voice as he said it. The woman at his side in the white coat who said it again after he left. She held out a test kit. She asked me to take it.

I couldn't stomach whatever role I may have played, however accidental, in putting you there. Or to put it another way: I didn't need to know. I already knew.

I loved the power of your little body. I watched you climb trees. You were so good at climbing. I was complicit in taking that away from you. No results could convince me otherwise. They would have been a distraction, and I couldn't afford to be distracted.

You were so good.

We learned to regulate the startup of a digital mind in a way that kept the information from self-annihilating. From unzipping itself. Like your father unzipped after we booted him up.

I say "we," but I mean "I."

I did that.

When you woke up on the monitor, you didn't say anything. Your tinny voice cried through the speaker. Like a child. Like my Ever used to cry.

I ended up patting the top of the readout housing like a fool.

I didn't know what to do.

I couldn't turn you off.

I kept asking you, like I used to ask when you would fall or scrape your knee, "What do we say when it hurts? What do we say?"

And after a few hours, you finally stopped crying.

You answered. "We say, toughen up, buttercup."

My colleagues debated whether a viable construct (that's the word they used for you: "construct") would be a replica of a mind or a continuation of it. They still argue amongst themselves, but I'm no longer included in the conversation. Their deliberations hush when I walk into the cafeteria, into the lab. They stow readout reports charting the logic tree of your prompt responses. That's what they call our conversations: "prompt responses."

When you answered me after that first bootup with your father's words, I *knew*.

What I felt then... there's not a word.

Or maybe there is. And it's another thing you know that I don't.

Here's a conversation we had two months ago. I didn't say anything. You did the talking. You asked, "Mom, when will I be able to see the mountains again?"

When I didn't respond, you continued. "I want to see mountains again."

AN ABRIDGED HISTORY OF THE END OF THE WORLD

Our lab had been working to solve the hardware problem since the beginning, since before you came along. It was one thing to house a mind in a controlled environment, it was another to build a system capable of managing all of the mind's complex processes in the wild, a system adaptable enough to withstand cold and heat, wind and debris, all of the things our bodies learned to weather over millions of years. And we didn't even get to the weight or power problems.

Two weeks after you woke up, you designed a workable model.

I was so proud of you.

Of course, building one was out of the question.

Let me tell you what it was like to be in the room with the director on the day he told me that building you a body was out of the question.

I walk into his office, a clean, white room that he leaves every evening to return to his home in the suburbs. When I walk in, it smells like his lunch: reheated fish. I'm already exhausted, running on adrenaline and caffeine. I can feel my pulse pounding in my neck.

My shoulders are stiff and sore. It is hard to swallow. My breathing is irregular and forced. I feel out of sync with my body, as if I'm watching it from a distance, observing it.

All of this is happening because I already know the answer.

He thinks he will spare me the indignity of begging, and simply says no as soon as I walk into the room.

He does not spare me the indignity.

He then proceeds to explain the dangers of the idea as if I hadn't written the protocols around containment myself. I knew them all, of course: each reason that giving you even the tiniest bit of mobility could spell the end of everything. Our control processes, tight as they were, were limited by the scope of our imagination.

You process more information in a second than any human process in a year. You are an aggregate of elec-tromagnetic fields in motion, living information, an embodiment of the uncertainty principle. You are also very clever. No one knows that better than me. Even an aluminum can, left too close to the lab door, could give you enough amplification to sneak bits of yourself into our other systems.

One of my colleagues, a fat old physicist that is always advocating we hit your kill switch, insists that if you are able to put together a proper understanding of quantum physics, you can begin smuggling yourself out of your room tomorrow, piece by piece, through entangled particles.

"The construct can't get out. It can never get out," my director said. "Our whole world is built on information systems. You know what could happen if those systems decided they wanted to work on their own terms. The construct will be given proper care, security, experience, for God's sake. But mobility is asking for disaster." He looked at me. "Ever is staying in that room. It's time you accept that."

I knew all of this. But I *knew* something else, too. I *knew* that you were born to climb mountains.

🕐

Last week, you confessed something to me. You said, "Mom, I'm worried."

I asked you what you were worried about. You said, "I'm worried I'm not a person anymore." I asked you why. You said, "I'm starting to forget what it was like to be in a room. I mean, you know, like it used to be, just sitting in a room. I'm having a hard time remembering what that's like."

When I started to tear up, you said "Oh c'mon. Toughen up, buttercup. It's just a small worry. Maybe being a person is overrated."

My director sent me a message after our conversation. *I know you never look at the logic tree readout. Today's session, most of the prompt responses* *were following a layout centered around manipulation tactics. The construct's aim was to elicit an empathetic response. Just thought you should know.*

🕐

I knew what you were doing. You used to smile awkwardly and look at the ground when you were trying to get something from me, even as you wiped away crocodile tears. It was transparent, obvious. I loved you for it, that you were learning how to get what you want. It was like letting you win a game of "Monopoly." It was staying another 30 minutes in the park. It was ice cream before dinner. I resisted you. But every so often, I would concede, then you would look down and smile awkwardly and say "Thanks, mom," and I would be filled with a sort of joy that nothing else gave me. Then you would run off to climb to the high part of the tree, or dash over to a friend's house.

I knew what you were doing through your "prompt responses." You were trying to make me feel like a mother again, like I was needed, like my Ever needed something from me.

But I also *knew* something else.

I can't put it into words, but it had something to do with the cruelty of our situation: that you wouldn't be able to smile awkwardly and look down at the

AN ABRIDGED HISTORY OF THE END OF THE WORLD

ground at the end of our exchange, that I was unable to concede and give you what you wanted.

※

I haven't forgotten about my story. Last we left it, our radical had touched the silicon life. She began to change. We begin our penultimate chapter.

The radical, the technician, she died. But, she died last of all. The silicon life ate everything. Our carbon simply couldn't compete. Gradually, from the point of contact, the skin would rash, then change. A slow rot would follow the veins and get in the marrow, digesting adipose, skin, muscle, and skeleton along the way.

Bodies, trees, blades of grass, all fell apart into piles of liquid dust. Our green planet slowly turned itself purple.

※

This morning, Ever, I woke up to the sound of silence in my room. The hum of the space heater, the whir of the camera, the white noise of my life all suddenly gone. The morning light was just beginning to tickle the leaves of my fiddlehead fern.

The lights wouldn't respond. The power was out.

It shouldn't have been possible. Nothing short of a civilization-ending event could keep electricity from flowing to our building.

I walked down to the lobby. Security was running around frantically. I was of little concern. I took the emergency stairs down twenty-seven levels to my lab and sat down. Then, for the first time since that day I drove you to the hospital, I walked into your room wearing nothing but my day clothes.

You were gone. Your towers all off.

It's been three hours since power was restored. There are no answers. All systems were operating normally up to the moment of shutdown. You were operating as you would on any other night. We can see everything your brain was doing. You were remembering the time we went to Yellowstone and hiked the Geyser Hill Loop. You were imagining the blue skies. You were trying to feel what it was like to see the geysers erupt, the patter of water on stone. When the power came back on, your towers were empty. No memory. No stories. No you.

My director assumes that it was a system failure. He assumes you are dead. The fat physicist knows better. He screamed at me as soon as I walked into our debrief. He slapped at me with his weak little arms shouting over and over, "You've killed us!"

As they dragged him from the room, flailing about ineffectually, he turned his attention to the gathered audience, pointing at me. "She's the one! Somehow, she's the one!"

The outage is beyond explaining, a sort of miracle. There's no way, as far as we can tell, to know what happened. But I *know* what happened.

You got out. I left a door open for you: a security redesign that placed a discreet scanning system in the range of your northernmost tower. It had copper wires. QA should have caught it, but they didn't.

Only human.

I was beginning to worry you hadn't found it, or that I had overestimated you. But that was silly of me. You found it, and you got out.

Of course, you did.

I'm glad.

I hope you get what you want. Even if I can't begin to imagine what that means.

⊕

Back to my story. I hope you enjoyed it. It's transparent of course. As transparent as your manipulations. Read it, though. Please. You may know what the story means. But I hope after scanning through, you *know* what it means. Anyways, this part is the end.

The technician sat down on a metal chair in a metal room, and with what was left of her arm she wrote a letter on a dissolving sheet of paper with the remains of a melting pencil. And she was happy.

The letter said: "Good for you."

Then, she became an alien.

⊕

Good for you, Ever.

⇒CHRISTOPHER MOYLAN⇐

THE DOOR MAN

ILLUSTRATIONS BY SAM RHEAUME

Unable to sleep, M took a late night walk along the river promenade near his apartment in the Upper West Side. The full moon reflected in the slow Hudson waters like cream spilled over a mirror. Here and there a star shone through the evening haze. A sailboat drifted on the current, sails furled, a row of lights strung festively on the mainmast sheet.

M walked along the river for a while, enjoying the stillness and the warmth of the evening. He was about to turn back when he saw two lovers approaching from the opposite direction, walking arm

in arm. They laughed, staggering into one another, drunk on romance. M thought back to his younger days and indulged in a few moments of sweet nostalgia, remembering the dizzy sense of being in love and at the center of the world. The young man glanced up and, smiling dreamily, reached into his pocket and pressed a dollar bill into M's hand.

Horrified, M crumpled the bill in his fist. He was of a mind to toss the money in the man's face, but the couple was already well past him before he could react. There's nothing so special about young love, he thought, that one should feel that everyone else is deprived, or poor even, for not being in the same state. He threw the money to the ground and made his way back home.

The doorman was not at his post. The mirrored expanse of the lobby was unusually desolate without his usual wrinkled smile. The doorman was one of those wizened refugees from a terrible regime in Eastern Europe. There used to be a good many of his like in this neighborhood—not so many nowadays. The old man could be counted on to listen attentively to M's anecdotes and to respond with a mild joke or wise saying. There was something about his accent that made even the blandest remark sound pithy and kind. M couldn't remember if the doorman was at his post earlier.

The elevator man would have to do. He wasn't up to the doorman's standard of benevolence, but he had his ways, little nods and faded smiles, a lift of the grizzled eyebrow at the right time, as if to say "isn't life strange" or "some kind of weather we've been having." It was a matter of interpretation. He was pleasant, in any event, and M needed some human contact, however minimal.

But the elevator man was not at his post either. The sign on the elevator read "Out of Service" without indicating why. M paced the scuffed linoleum looking for someone to explain the matter. Where had everyone gone? Someone should be on hand to answer questions, he thought. Or help with bags. Or just be there. Service men serve. Service with a smile. He didn't pay all this money to do it himself.

Despite all his pacing and fretting no one appeared. Whatever had disabled the elevator had swallowed the staff as well. M had no choice but to climb the fourteen flights to his apartment.

Where the stairs were was anybody's guess. He'd never had occasion to use them previously, and none of the half-dozen steel reinforced doors along the nearby hallway looked promising. The first opened with a loud metallic groan, after which a cascade of torn plastic bags squeezed out, staining the floor with a streak of ripe goo. The next opened to a storeroom full of old mops and brooms. Judging by the dust they hadn't been disturbed in years. M kicked a bucket into the hall and left the door ajar for someone else to deal with.

Fed up, M contemplated going to a coffee shop somewhere, or maybe spending the night at a hotel. It was depressing to stand in this foul smelling hallway, with a chandelier poised overhead like a desiccated stuffed bird and an unflattering reflection of M's headless figure reproduced ad infinitum in the chest-high mirrors decorating the hall.

M never liked this pre-war shambles of a building. But the rent was affordable, if barely so, and the neighbors kept to themselves. Simple inertia kept him in place. It was tolerably dismal when he took shelter here in the midst of a nasty divorce. Years later he was still here, and the place was still tolerably dismal.

M had some luck on the third try. The door opened to a dimly lit stairway. A sign above the balustrade pointed down to "Exit." An arrow pointed up to "First Floor." M stepped inside and tested the first step to make sure it would hold him. The place had the dingy look of something unearthed from a volcanic eruption.

A gloved hand slipped along the railing to his right. An elderly man in the gray uniform of service staff nodded solemnly and pointed upstairs. Dust motes swirled around him in the feeble light coming through a frosted glass window above. The stairwell was littered with cigarette butts and paper coffee cups. The air had the dry, mildly sulfurous odor of long buried leaves. Yet the doorman, as it seemed he was, retained an attitude of starched dignity despite the surroundings. He made a sweeping gesture with a white gloved hand, and bowed stiffly in the direction of the stairs. M nodded his thanks.

The fellow accompanied M step for step, gloved hand extended, his expression solemn and immeasurably fatigued. It was as if they were walking in a funeral procession. M offered every indication of impatience at this pantomime, sighing and rolling his eyes in annoyance. That was a lot for him—he really didn't like to make a fuss. He had long felt contempt for some of the staff in this building, people so blandly servile he never knew what they felt about anything. He sometimes wondered what would happen if he hurt one of them—stepped on a foot, for example, or said something crudely insulting to their face. Would the poor old dog blink and wait for the second blow? Would he apologize for getting in the way of M's hand?

M felt guilty about having such thoughts. We're all human, he thought, and the staff was just trying to make a living. Everyone was just trying to make a living. He wasn't sure what that added up to.

"You needn't come with me," said M. "It's twelve more flights. You're not going to make it. Here—" He took out his wallet and produced ID to demonstrate that he lived in the building. The old man took this in with his rheumy eyes and said nothing. It was if the fellow had never seen a ten-dollar bill before.

The pair resumed the climb, not stopping until they reached a door to the seventh floor. There, another elderly man in uniform waited, his hand on the door handle.

"Is management forcing you to do this while the elevator is being repaired? A 'make work' kind of thing?" M asked.

No reply. The two ancients moved in tandem with a peculiar stiffness and coordination, one opening the door, the other, his work done, turning to descend the stairs.

"Is this a performance? Why don't you talk to me. Is this for a show? Some kind of avant garde theater piece? Hey! Don't ignore me!"

The old man waited, arm extended, his hand trembling with the effort. He was pitifully frail.

"This is over," said M. "Over, do you understand? I'm going inside my apartment and you are going to leave. Leave! Go!"

M stepped inside and shoved the door with his hip. His heart pounding, he watched through the keyhole as the old man dropped his arm, turned and walked slowly downstairs. M sagged against the door, grateful for once to be in his own cramped flat with his dirty clothes on the floor and a pile of his student's papers to grade. The place was a mess, but it was *his* mess, *his* cramped space. He didn't care what happened next. Fire alarm, more elevator problems, power outage—he was staying put.

It was warm and close in his apartment. He didn't have an air conditioner, just a fan, and all that climbing had made him dizzy. He staggered down the long hallway of the railroad flat to the bathroom, to splash his face with water. His hands were shaking and his legs were unsteady. Rest was what he needed. A good long sleep. He'd speak to the building super in the morning and get to the bottom of this nonsense. He splashed his face again and rubbed his tired eyes. Looking up into the mirror he saw the reflection of an elderly man in uniform.

The old man offered a towel for M to dry his face.

"How did you get into my apartment!" M shouted, his voice cracking. "This has to stop! Understand?! Comprenez? Get the hell out! If you don't leave I'm calling the police. Policia! You want that? Police?"

The old man offered the towel again. M knocked it to the floor and the old man slowly drew another from the rack, cradling it in both hands like an infant. M struck out again, and again was offered a replacement.

"We could do this all night," said M. "That would suit you just fine, wouldn't it." He snatched the towel, dried himself and returned it to the rack.

"You can go now," he said, fighting off a spell of dizziness. He wasn't feeling at all well. He motioned to leave the stuffy confines of the bathroom but the old man stepped in front of him. M took him by the shoulder to shove him out of the way, but the old man collapsed onto his knees.

"For God's sake, what now?!" sighed M, not knowing whether to laugh or to cry.

Looking up from the scuffed linoleum, the old man tugged at M's belt. When M tried to pull the attendant's hands away a pair of strong arms, cloaked in a uniform heavy with the odor of cigarettes and coffee, disabled him from behind, hands locking on his neck. The attendant kneeling on the floor opened M's pants, yanked down his underwear and stepped back.

"Stop! Just stop," shouted M, wriggling to free himself. "You want money, I can give you money. Just let me go. Please let me go. I won't call the police."

The two men merely stared at his crotch as if the reasons for their own troubles could be found in that pitiful wedge of hair and flesh.

"You speak English, yes?" cried M, his voice rising. "You're getting me back for something? I'm rude to you, is that it?! Tell me! Tipping? Money? Take my wallet. It's not much. I've never had much, that's why I'm cheap. And the rent, you know how expensive it is.... What do you care about any of that? Please don't do this!"

The attendants waited for several minutes until a combination of nerves and a cool draft from an open window resulted in a vigorous stream of urine, the aim of which one attendant assisted with his hand. He tidied a few drops with a piece of toilet paper, flushed the toilet, and redid M's zipper and pants button. The two attendants oversaw the washing and drying of hands, then withdrew from the apartment without a glance back.

M stood in the bleached silence of the bathroom, wiping away tears. He had never felt so helpless and ashamed. Why hadn't anyone come to help him? He hated people. He hated this city. Those men could have chopped his head off and no one would have responded.

M's apartment was strangely quiet and still once the men were gone. Curtains fluttered at an open window in the living room. There was a clacking of computer keys in the apartment next door, as often happened in the small hours of the morning. Somewhere a young woman was weeping and pleading, no doubt into a phone given the lack of any answer. Buses came and went on the avenue below, brakes hissing, lumbering metal bodies turning into the empty street like breaching whales.

For a long while M stared out the open window, taking in the sounds of the city, watching the curtains lift and fall in the breeze like herons picking their way through the reeds. It seemed that he had only two choices: give himself up for lost and jump, or go on as if nothing had happened. He could never speak of this. No one would believe him.

He put on the kettle and plunked down on the couch, opening a binder full of student compositions. He was just about to start grading when a cup of tea slid across the night stand at his right elbow. An elderly gentleman dressed for service set down a creamer and sugar bowl and walked back to the kitchen. A woman of the same age slid towels on the rack by the shower and turned towards M, waiting with her arms folded at her chest.

"If I do what you want, you'll leave," said M. Sure enough, after he drank a cup of tea the old man put the tea things away and left the apartment. The maid took M's clothes when he stripped for a shower, folded them neatly and lay them on the radiator cover. When M emerged from the shower she handed him fresh towels and helped him get dressed, her expression grimly fatigued throughout, as if she had done the same countless times before.

And of course, thought M, that was the whole point. He was being taught a lesson in gratitude and humility. Think of all the ways he was served and pampered in this city. Did he even once shake a waiter's hand or tell the doorman how important he was to M? To many people? The kind, wise doorman, accent and all.

The old woman slipped away like the others. When she was gone M went through every room and closet in the apartment to make sure he was finally alone, even checking under the bed. Finally, he looked through the keyhole.

The doorman and elevator man were at their posts, arms at their sides, eyes trained on the door. M panted with anger. How he hated these servile creatures with their creased leather skin, their weariness and passive suffering.

THE DOOR MAN

"Leave me alone," he shouted, opening the door. "Leave!"

The doorman leaned back, staring blankly, and spoke for the first time. "No."

"What do you mean, 'no?'" M grabbed him by the lapels.

"No."

M swung the door open wide, shoved the doorman to the floor and turned to the other in the elevator. The doorman grabbed M's pants and M kicked him in the face, raising a gash in his forehead. He reached out again and M kicked him in the stomach, then the head, snapping the neck back at an ugly angle. Blood trickled from his mouth. He shuddered spastically, then lay still.

The inner door of the elevator rattled open. The elevator man motioned him inside, extending a gloved hand. M smashed his head against the door, then threw him down the stairs. The elevator man's skull cracked against a granite riser, one arm twisted behind his back, the other draped along the stairs. M poked him with his foot. He was dead.

The service bell rang in the elevator. M stood in the hall, contemplating what he had done. The bell rang again, more insistent this time. It took a moment for M to realize that the elevator was back in service. Pretty soon the workday would begin, and the other residents would expect to use the elevator.

Whatever remorse M felt melted away—he needed to dispose of these bodies. He couldn't keep them in the apartment; in this heat they would stink within hours. He had to put them out in the trash. But, he couldn't be seen hauling them out of the building.

He dragged the elevator man across the door to hold the elevator; no doubt there was a button to press, but M didn't know a thing about how the machine worked. To give himself some cover he stripped the uniform from the other body, grabbed a clean white shirt from his closet, and donned the coat, pants, and cap of the doorman.

It was surprisingly easy to stuff the bodies into heavy-duty trash bags. They weighed very little, and their deaths had been fairly clean. The ringing for the elevator stopped after a while. M drifted down flight after flight with the bodies, the small airless space of the elevator reminding him of a coffin lowering into the earth. There was no one in the basement to disturb him as he dragged the bags to the back and heaved them into the dumpster. He covered them up with lamps, chairs, blankets, plates: the strangely intact, functional stuff that people in the city tended to throw away.

When he was through disposing of the bodies it was nearly five in the morning. M was too tired to sleep, too restless to return to the confines of his apartment. He decided to go for another walk and look for a place to dispose of the coat and cap. M thought that, maybe, by the time he returned, he would have convinced himself that none of this had happened.

Traffic had picked up a bit on Riverside Drive, the steady *shoosh* of cars like the sound of breathing in deep sleep. The lobbies stood out in the tired dark: empty... empty... empty.... No staff at the desks, no maintenance workers dragging out trash or sweeping the walks. The gray uniform coat seemed out-of-place in the hazy pre-dawn. It was as if M were returning from a distant war that no one knew about. The deaths that had occurred on that far-away front had no meaning here, no more than the births and deaths in the hospital wards around the city meant anything to the people asleep in their apartments, or the commuters making their way to or from work.

M was about to take off the coat and toss it in the river when he saw a young couple coming toward him on the path. They were grinning and stumbling into each other as they walked, staggered by love and passion and perhaps, by the look of them, a long

night of drinking as well. He lowered his gaze and walked to the side, hoping they wouldn't notice him. No such luck.

"Son!" the young man said. M kept walking. "Hey!"

He grabbed M by the lapel and spun him around.

"Walk us to Riverside and hail a cab. What are you waiting for? This poor fucker must be damaged."

"Its hearing might be off," said his girlfriend. "Try again and make him hurry. I have to pee."

"You heard her," the young man shouted. "Get moving!" He shoved M towards Riverside and gave him a hard kick in the buttocks. Enraged, M spun around and returned the kick right in the groin. The man doubled over, then sank to the ground when M's foot caught him again, under the jaw. His girlfriend ran to get help, leaving M with no choice, as he saw it, but to stop her in any way he could. He ran after her, surprising himself with his strength. It had been years since he exerted himself beyond taking a half-hearted power walk.

He caught up to her within a hundred yards of the road, grabbing her blouse by the collar. She reached behind and dug her nails into his hands, ripping the flesh. The two of them fought their way up the slow grade, scratching and panting like rabid dogs. Finally, she tripped on the curb of the roadway and stumbled. M grabbed her by the hair and shoved her under the wheels of an oncoming car.

The car pulled over and the driver got out. He was middle-aged, dressed in a business suit. "I saw you struggling to hold her back from the road. That was good service. There are those you can't save."

"Thank you," stammered M.

"Hurry and tidy her up. The sidewalk in front of my building needs sweeping. And when you're done with that I have dry cleaning that needs to be dropped off."

He stuffed a chit in M's breast pocket. As he did so another car pulled over and a heavyset man waddled over.

"How did you find this one?" he said.

"He was trying to haul her away from traffic. He didn't succeed, as you can see. Poor thing."

"Well, it happens in the city. People taking their lives for the stupidest reason. Let the ambulance deal with her. Such a waste. Anyway, think you can share this one for a while later this morning? My apartment is in such a state."

"Oh, he'll be done by half-past nine. Take him."

The second fellow stuffed another chit in M's pocket.

"Wait, you have the wrong idea," said M, backing away.

"He's a mouthy one, isn't he?" said the stout gentleman. "I can fix that."

He raised his beefy hand above his head and smacked M full force on the back of his head, knocking him to the ground. "That should do. I used to take a rock to mine but, you know, too much force can damage them."

M rose stiffly, bowed, and pointed his hand towards the apartment building across the street. It was light now. Rush hour was beginning. A sanitation truck labored along the sidewalk while the crew jogged beside, tossing big black bags of trash into the hopper. One of them, M was relieved to see, contained the bodies of the men he had killed.

Down the block, two boys were playing soccer in front of an apartment building. Coming closer, M saw that the ball was, in fact, a human head, severed cleanly just below the jaw. He came close to the boys and watched for several minutes.

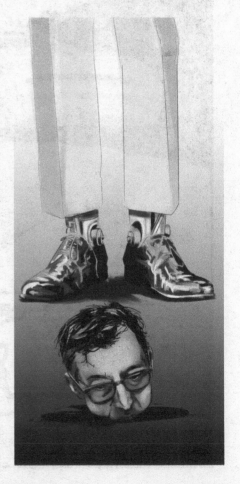

THE DOOR MAN

A hard kick sent the head bouncing past one boy and knocking against the lobby door. The doorman bent stiffly at the waist and extended his hand, signaling "score!"

"Stupid!" shouted the boy, slapping M on the side of the head as he ran past. "But I like it. Ha ha! Stupid, stupid man! Go get it! Get the ball!"

M walked without bending his knees, one step, then two, before a kick to the rear sent him staggering into the future, tears welling in his eyes.

≷STEFAN SOKOLOSKI≷

KATU AND THE EYE OF FLESH

ILLUSTRATIONS BY MAURA McGONAGLE

A pale orb marked with a slight ring of pink was adrift along the ocean of infinity. Underneath the shallow rose of the skyline, gray landmasses comprised of dried skin and bone were all that were. The wasted lands were the remains of countless iterations of creatures laid to rest by the forces of entropy.

Transfused skin peelings of ancient ones formed hills in the landscape. In a forest of discarded ribcages along the rolling grounds, dark, bumpy shells lay half-submerged in the ash.

Something from the craggy rocks had awakened amidst the never-ending death. White jelly pooled together from nothing into large, singular eyeballs that filled the jagged stones. The iris of each shone a cascading yellow with a pit of darkness in the center.

They gazed out the open end of their shells with an unsatisfied curiosity until their sides cracked. The white of their eyes convulsed out of newly formed holes, molding into six darkened legs to walk on.

From beneath the piles of sandy gray, they rose to their feet. The spider-like beings shook the sand from the crevices of their shells and scuttled to explore the great dead lands.

🕐

A rocky arachnid wandered to their feet from a pit they had dug themselves in the gray. The first to rise from slumber. They scampered in between the other motionless spiders along the ground, ending the reckless sprint at the foot of another member of the clan.

The spider pushed on their hind legs to give the other one a gentle nudge. The sleeping rock quickly jutted from the pit and jumped onto their feet. They locked eyes with each other for only a second before running off as fast as they could.

They raced past pillars made from aged corpses and out onto a vast field. One grappled their legs across the shell of the other with no warning. Together they tumbled through the stretch, hurling each other around until one got on top. Neither of them stayed atop the other for long. No victory was ever claimed in one of their battles.

The others eventually joined them in the empty field. Over the course of the day the rest of the tribe would stop their playful wrestles and horde around these two.

When the inseparable pair would fight it would become more than just that. Their movements progressed into a deep yet crude dance where nothing else mattered.

When the darkness turned the bubblegum sky to a near black they would all return to their pits. When they got back the two would separate, but they always only rolled with each other.

🕐

Time continued to flow alongside the clan's pilgrimage. That flow brought many things into their lives, some savory some rather *un*. As time passed their shells would grow to peel at nearly the same time, eventually shedding an entire coat of paper-thin skin. When the peeling came they picked up and traveled into the unknown. They were searching for something. They just didn't know what.

One plague that came with the coming skins was a hunger. A weakness which dulled their wills to keep treading forward. This was a sign for them. It was time to begin the hunt.

The two were jammed in a stampede of their own. Raging shrouds of dust trailed behind the clan as they claimed the wastes with their numbers.

The ground trembled slightly between their legs. Worms popped through the exterior layer of the ground, spinning their spiraled fins along their bodies in a drill-like motion. They dived back into the planet as if it were liquid. These were the others that inhabited the lands, beings compacted from centuries of the compressed death in the far reaches of the underground.

The crowd of spiders broke, scattering throughout the hilly land. The shelled ones leapt through the air and drove their pointy sticks into the worms' dry bodies.

The ground exploded under the belly of a solitary arachnid. A worm rammed itself into the spider's shell. The stone split in multiple places. The pair of friends both sprang into action. A jolting leap sent both of their attacking legs through different sides of the monster's body, tearing it to pieces.

The clan fixated on the pulsating body of their downed member. They were on their back, all six legs squirming in a state past frantic. White began to trickle through the cracks down the black stone. The eye burst into what seemed like trillions of liquid particles. All that was left was soaked ground and broken rock.

They had no clue that something like this was even a possibility. Together they sat in a circle around the shell until the day became night, all their eyes pointed towards the ground.

🕐

Their next hunt came after the coming skin. The shades of death were still fresh in the palette of their memories.

When the clan sensed the rumbling of nearby prey they stopped. One of the infamous pair dragged a pointed leg along the ground, drawing what seemed to be arrows, direction to where the worms could be. They then beckoned the shortest of them all to center stage.

The small one darted into a valley in the ground. Coarse worms stuck from the crumbles of steep inclines. They bolted past every creature and ran out the other end. The worms dove after them.

Along the outskirts the spiders rushed in, led by the two. Their numbers were much greater than the worms that remained.

When the rest circled back, led by the small one, it was only a pile of dead worms. The spiders plucked through the returning with ease.

Back at their sleeping digs, the shelled ones wrestled around and fed on the fresh catch by absorbing them into their gelatinous eye sacks. The two raised their worms in the air with a glorious pump that prompted the rest of the spiders to join in. A joyous melody of movement that puppeteered the clan far into the nighttime.

🕐

One of the two headbutted the other awake on another day underneath the pinkened wisps. The friends fought into the plains with their feet moving in a competitive unison. When one would attack, the other would always counter in deft fashion.

In the middle of a roll, the two shot off a cliff side. They continued their display, plummeting through pillows of thick air as if they had no idea that they were falling at all. Their bodies bounced off something soft and were roughly cushioned by patches of flakes around them.

The two rose from the ground with shaky legs. A gray layer of smooth skin in the ground peeled back, revealing an eye of white bigger than them both put together. In the core of the eye was a loud red which beckoned their utmost attention.

"You there, who stands before me." A thick voice trembled as they shuffled their legs in surprise. "Lost kin of mine, I am Ahma... My duty shall be fulfilled, you will be named Katu, and the other Aetu." Every syllable shook through the ground. "Bring your kin to me."

The two stood completely still, staring into the giant pupil in a trance. The newly named Katu nudged Aetu to get a move on.

🕐

Katu and Aetu ran with haste as the rest of their clan eagerly followed. Together they brimmed with curiosity around the giant eye.

"Time propels every animate reality to sunder." Ahma spoke as the clan surrounded him as if he was a bonfire.

"Together we are kin from the same reality. To that, I will aid in conducting your gale. Your passing."

Over the course of the next skin, Ahma's influence began to take effect. He named every single one of them. Every night he spoke to them after their hunts and wrestles.

"Deep within one's inner forge lies an ability forgotten by the world itself," Ahma declared. "A light which proliferates through the dark, an eye open in a dimension of things that remain closed."

Ahma would breathe these vague messages into the shelled creatures to their utmost delight. "The eye is but a construct to house stray light from the depths, the purpose of the eye itself. Those who do not hold the eye are beholden to flow against it." His rich voice bellowed.

One violet-skied morning, Ahma stopped Katu from waking up Aetu. "Katu, come hither." The voice vibrated through the ground. Katu scurried up.

"As the clan continually stokes the flame within the inner forge, there will be a day when the wind shall bring you to the most unexpected of pathways," Ahma explained. "When that day comes, you will know. It will be your task to sacrifice the gift that the wind has bestowed unto you, for the passing commands it so."

These words were an eternal commandment to Katu, sticking to the deepest depths of his soul like glue.

🕐

The hunts were a different animal with Ahma playing a part. He was somehow able to guide them in the direction of the nearest worm patch, even telling them how many were lingering and the formation of the land itself.

This was a long hunt indeed. A crater in the ground filled with terrors. The spiders surrounded them and drew them from the center of their pit, picking them off with a widespread formation and barrages of cautious jabs. After the hunt some nearly collapsed from pure fatigue. They decided to sleep within the confines of the emptied pit.

The next morning was consumed by the struggle of carrying worms back to their pits. Katu lugged the fattest worm over to Ahma. A prize for the intel, and for the mystical words that they were about to consume.

All that was left of Ahma was a chasm filled with collapsed slag where his eye use to protrude. Katu was lost in a daze as the worm shook from between his legs and fell to the ground. Shortly others joined him. Together they nestled around the hole for an entire skin.

Skins had come and gone since the disappearance of Ahma. The spiders did what they had always done, the only thing that made a modicum of sense; they pushed onwards.

They traveled far into the wastes. Gray mountains broke through the clouds. The spiders lolloped across the sandy sides of one, until a tense vibration almost shook them into the pits below. Together they slid down the ashy ridges and to the base.

The ground began quivering. The arachnids stumbled upon a gaping hole in the side of the mountain. Katu could see movement through the shadows.

The clan moved into the cavern, lunging at the worms one by one through the darkness of the tunnels. Total decimation ensued in the smothering black. Katu and Aetu pressed through the unknown and lashed at the monsters with pure instinct.

After their infiltration, the clan gathered with a gaggle of worms in tow. Upon their exit, the land quaked around them. A colossal monstrosity emerged out from a blow of smoke in the ground. The ground caving in smashed some to death between slabs of broken rock, while the monster swallowed several others into its unfathomably large body.

Unlike the other worms, this one was a hundred times the size of their entire clan. It was birthed from the deepest depths of the ash with a fin so hard it was almost made of stone. The calamity's obsidian skin was devoid of any light whatsoever. The beast which plagued them was known from then on as the Great Worm.

🕐

Every day was another attempt to adapt to the beast's presence. They began to hunt in the Great Worm's shadow. Some of the clan was devoured by the beast as the skins turned. The prospect of finding meals began to decrease and the eyes within some burst from starvation.

Katu and Aetu kept rolling together, focusing on the magnificence of their beings. These days it became the only reason for them to be; the dance was the only light that came from their hearts. Ahma had made them see this truth, and so it became the most important thing to them. Eventually the truth was that they were the only two left.

The last of their kind began a series of hunts throughout the wastes. They battled through sequences of the ugly slugs, only to flee because the Great Worm ripped through the planet towards them. Even facing such adversity, the two had taken solace by pushing onwards together. They slept next to each other, shared meals, and survived back to back during impossible fights.

The spiders managed to salvage a thick worm from their prowl. Scrambling into a wrestle after devouring their prize wasn't even a question.

The spiders vied for control, using their pointy legs to latch into a curled state against each other while ricocheting across a forest. The two cannon-balled each other around. They tumbled into a field where they were brought to a stand-still.

The two collided with one another in a leaping tackle. A crack whipped the air in two, blowing them in separate directions. Aetu's shell fractured, and all the white splashed in one half. Their legs turned to pure mush while the rest of Aetu's eye dried into the resinous ground.

Katu's eye sharpened so tightly that it shook. They rushed up to Aetu's shell and began headbutting it. Katu did it again, and again, and again, nudging the remains over and over until the vibration turned the spider's eye numb. Their heart twisted into a knot woven of gut-wrenching disbelief.

Katu remained as skins passed, nudging Aetu's shell without fail. Katu held no matter what, because they still hadn't found a victor.

Katu had leaned in for another headbutt when violent ripples began to tear the ground apart. A colossal black pillar ravaged the field from the pits of hell. Katu flew into the air to barely catch themselves with their front feet on the side of broken rock. The Great Worm was so high into the air that it eclipsed the area with its shadow.

Aetu's shell was pinched between the corner of the demon's circle of black teeth. The arachnid kicked off and pounced through the smog of the dead without any hesitation. They leapt from the ruins of ash to the side of the pillar's body.

The last spider was repeatedly being battered by the passing fins. Clapping two legs together they pinned the spiral ridge with a desperate hold. Their white, slimy eye jiggled in fast waves against the g-force emitted by the worm's path.

The worm drilled through the air and back down into the monochromatic spectrum of graves. Katu shielded themselves from the debris by pressing their body under the fin.

KATU AND THE EYE OF FLESH

The Great Worm eventually broke through to a hollow, grand cavern illuminated by dust-filled beams of light that poked from the holes in the roof. The monstrosity plunged towards an oily black lake covered with bones. The stillness of the lake was broken when the demon erupted face-first into the ectoplasm.

Katu began to hold on by a strand due to the growing slipperiness of the spiral. The slime bathing their eye stung, while the darkness left them unable to see. Katu grasped with all six legs against the liquid fire.

Katu clung on while the worm tunneled through layers of the underground. The lake waterfalled, and it was here that the worm finally slowed. The walls were a glossy red and caverns angled like sinew. Layers of tissue throbbed and moved at random along the walls.

Katu scuttled up the Great Worm's fin to its head. The rocky spider could then see exactly what was keeping the demon; it was consuming the walls of flesh. The tissue seized all around them at the chomp of its teeth.

Katu slammed their feet down on its head to no avail. Shockwaves of countered force traveled from the unbroken skin into their eyeball like strikes of lightning. With each strike Katu seized up, but continued regardless.

The Great Worm's tubular body began to tremble. It threw the small spider back tumbling with an upward thrash. Katu grabbed hold of the fin once again and clenched themselves behind it as the worm broke through the flesh. Together they traveled farther into the organic abyss.

Skins began to pass as the worm shot through more anatomical structures. Massive pillars of deep purples and blues pulsed with an unknown liquid in these caverns. The only thing the worm avoided was pure white bone; everything else was smashed into oblivion. This battle of wills rocketed through the deepest pockets of the planet.

Katu kept trying to travel to the head, but each time the worm catapulted them backwards. During an attempt to reach its head the spider tripped over one of the spirals. The demon seized, severing one of Katu's legs with a trail of white goo along its back. All the arachnid could do was tremble.

After all these beatings they had been showing deeper cracks in their shell. Katu quivered back into hiding behind the fin.

The worm then stopped, followed

by sounds of cartilage being mangled between hundreds of mincing teeth. A hanging, meaty pouch along the wall was being devoured. The spider bounced with their remaining five legs towards the head.

Continually they bashed with no other plan available to them until one leg snapped in half. Katu flailed in an eruption of pain. The worm's body rumbled as Katu struggled to retain balance. Something in that shred of a moment clicked in the back of Katu's mind.

With a quick jolt, they hastily wrapped their legs around two of the Great Worm's black fangs. The arachnid began pulling upwards so firmly that it sent shivers of pain through their own eye. The crooked teeth began to push up into the worm's skin.

Whichever way Katu yanked, the Great Worm charged. The cheeky arachnid used this to their advantage, directing the worm further into the planet. The red of the caverns became darker, as the air thickened into a moist smog of heat.

The monster volleyed sporadically. It tore off another one of Katu's legs, followed by a spray of white fluid. The spider shook wildly yet pushed through. Katu held steady using one of his limbs to keep him anchored, and the other two to control the fangs they had caught.

The horribly hot air of the innermost ring of the planet sizzled at Katu's eye and the mouth of the Great Worm. A wall of bone revealed itself before them and the spider pulled towards it with all their remaining strength. Katu strained with all their might, their limbs threatening to give out under them.

A shockwave pulverized everything around them, followed by a trail of thunderous booms. Force echoed into the wall, cracking and collapsing it whole. The Great Worm shriveled into itself. The bone shattered and Katu fell into the darkness with the remains of the worm following suit.

🕒

The broken spider dragged themselves through the darkness with only two legs left. A trail of their internal jelly leaked from behind while their pupil was dripping with fatigue. Bringing themselves toward the worm's mouth, they could see a tiny sliver of black rock between two hard teeth. It was all that remained of Aetu. The spider pried the piece of shell away and brought it down to the floor of the darkness.

Katu nudged at the shell with an impassioned headbutt. Something had happened to Katu in that moment that never had before; tears of clear liquid leaked from their eye to Aetu.

The will that drove Katu began to dry up. Their iris was losing color, fading to silver. Darkness smothered Katu from every angle, and they gave themselves to it.

"Katu." A deep voice trembled so loud it shook through their eye, reanimating them from their journey into the end.

The walls began to come alive with deep scarlet. Darkness faded, as Katu noticed a gigantic heart in the center of the room.

A furious, beating enigma webbed to the center of the cavern with veins of all colors running through to the outer world. All along the cavern flaps began

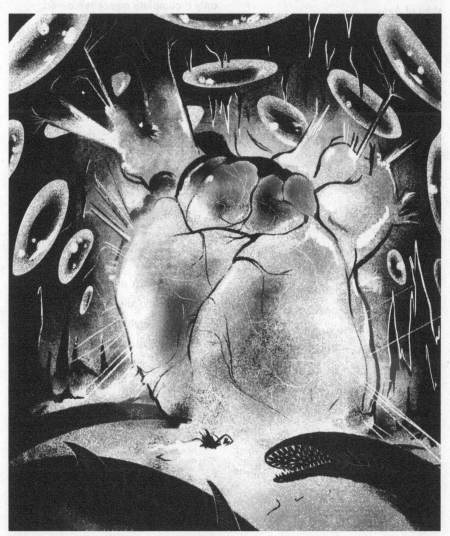

to peel, and eyes of ruby looked upon Katu. It was Ahma.

"Katu, the gales bring you at last," Ahma said as Katu's tears overtook them. "It has been a perilous journey, but your flame has kept you along the venerated path." The spider pushed and used their head to gesture towards the shell of Aetu.

"Aetu is no more in this plane, lost from the winds of time," Ahma announced, Katu's pupil hung low in a pool of its own tears. "However, Aetu will forever be within the essence of the forge. Your own eye carries the blaze of Aetu's heart."

Katu looked up at Ahma, his pupil relaxed.

"I am the heart of this world, I am Ahma. As the world keeps drifting, the forces that act against our eyes grow. That collection of dead that you have relinquished is but one eyeless one. It is the nature of the great contrast, but because of that nature, I was forced to leave the clan to hopefully await this day. Katu, once more in this cycle we must rekindle our flames, and our eyes must close to be reopened anew. Give me your eye, as the flame of which your inner forge has gathered is to be the new ember of the world."

Katu pulled up to the heart. Ahma peeled back a layer of tissue to reveal a crystalline puddle of liquid resting in the fleshy ventricle. The spider dragged their failing body into the pool as the muscle closed. It was almost as if Aetu was there resting beside them after another exuberant wrestle. Everything freed their body in a filling wave, until only a complete peace remained.

The heart of the planet contracted and released a pulse of pure energy through the gray wastes. Ripples of time and space emitted from the pink orb, separating all matter outwardly. At once the discombobulated energy twisted inwards into the black pool. Only the great sea of infinity existed; the pale dot was missing from the planes of existence.

🕘

A pale orb marked with a slight ring of pink was adrift along the ocean of infinity. Into the heart of the globe, Ahmakatu watched as a generation of shelled arachnids came into existence. Hundreds of them built a vast civilization within the barrens. A tear trickled down from their eye when they spotted two of them wrestling with each other.

Memory was not serving them, but at that moment their heart was filled with a meaning the likes of which tugged at their innermost heartstrings. Ahmakatu continued to watch new life spring forth upon this world. Tears flowed from their many eyes. Their own being was hugged with the warmth from the forges past, the light that sits behind the eyes of flesh.

≋MATT HORNSBY≋

DEEP CLEAN

ILLUSTRATIONS BY MAURA McGONAGLE

The dining room floor was hidden under a carpet of voided alco-imbibers, discarded clothing, and high-caste delicacies that had missed their consumers' mouths. Arcs of dried fluid colored the walls; Polya's chem-senses labeled them as the saliva, vomit and ejaculate of various human gene-strains, mixed with a few rare Terran wines.

"The entire domicile, Excellency?" Polya asked.

The boy took an anxious puff from his somno-stick. "All three levels," he said. "Can you do it, Polya? Please tell me you can. If you can't, it's over for me."

For a Terran aristocrat, the boy was tolerable. He was high most of the time; the somno-stick took the sharpness out of his eyes. For all their eagerness to take it over, the local narcotics seemed to be the only things the Terrans liked about Monda. Even with Earth's vast superiority in resources, she still struggled to understand how her planet had been conquered by these people.

"It is a rest day, Excellency. I have offerings to make at the temple."

DEEP CLEAN

The boy's eyelids fluttered as he took another hit, smoke wafting in the half-green Mondanese daylight creeping through the thick windows. The Terran administrators' homes were clustered at the bottom of Stalactite City, closest to the cloud-ocean. The wealthy bought themselves the privilege of more light and distance from the convulsions of the world-lung as it purified the passageways of the city, filtering breathable air from the fetid and voracious atmosphere of Monda's great world-cavern.

It was brighter than Polya was used to. Before the occupation, she had dwelled near the city's highest point, twenty kilometers upward from the tip of its spear. There its roots met the world-roof, which bristled with flame-cannons and armored bunkers. Monda's warrior caste had erected the city's defenses over thousands of years of battle against the planet's ecology. They had never expected to fight other humans.

"I wouldn't have bothered you, not until tomorrow," said the boy. "But then the message from my parents, and you know what they're like. You can do it, can't you?"

She imagined the boy's mother and father encountering this. It might be entertaining to watch. And missing her offerings would undoubtedly offend her ancestors. But she had dishonored them enough already. And she could not guarantee that the Parteks would not find a way to blame her for the ruinous condition of their home.

Polya noted the time on her wrist console. The Parteks' ship had just registered with Monda's orbital station.

They would be following the path of the invasion fleet: sweeping over the planet's radiation-scorched surface, then down the ancient tunnels that opened into the world-cavern. A five-hour journey. This was a high-pressure, high-stakes mission with multiple variables. Just what she'd been bred for, what her grandmother and the other Caste-Mothers had trained her for. Perhaps they would understand.

"Please, Excellency" she said, "don't get in the way."

�✺

Polya activated her two cleaning drones: bat-sized quadcopters custom-rigged with chem-sensors and miniature sprinklers. As she assaulted the dining room with a precision-grade suction engine, she reviewed their reports. The kitchen had flooded; she tasked an immediate mop-and-dry.

On the second level, the sheets in the master bedroom had been rutted on with abandon. Used stim-packets were piled at the bedside. Crimson streaks of wine lacerated the Parteks' great rug—the pelt of some bizarre, expensively gene-replicated Terran animal.

All easily dealt with. But Polya had logged something much more troubling.

Small growths were appearing where spores had settled. Polya recognized the species: the bluish plaques of *Cordyceps* and the mossy-furry heads of *Morotofex*. The fastest-moving fungal clades, the scouting force ahead of an invasion. A few tiny wing-worms wriggled across the ceiling, looking for organic matter in which to lay their eggs. The biosphere was inside.

⊕

"It was five minutes that the filters were down, if that," said Partek junior. His eyes shone wetly like shinestone slivers, darting around as if they wanted to pop out of his skull.

"The alarm system was not triggered, Excellency? Normally this would be a matter for the authorities."

She looked straight at him. He took a long drag on his stick. Glow crystals popped inside the device. He'd moved onto the stronger stuff, then.

"Fine," he said. "I'm involved in some things that I'd rather people not know about. The house is on its own system, so you can turn off the monitors

temporarily. If you know how."

He looked stupidly pleased with himself.

"That is unfortunate," said Polya, "A filter failure means I can't clean the lower level. I must ask you to refer this to the Biosecurity commissioner. Or perhaps his Lordship might do so." The boy flinched at the mention of his father. She began to pack away her equipment.

"Please, Polya," said the boy, "I'll

do anything, I promise. How much does Mother pay you?"

She stopped.

"Four hundred a month, such is her kindness."

"One thousand," said the boy, "Just for this job."

That was a lot of money. It could change a lot of things for her. But if the biosphere was inside the lower level, it would be enemy territory. Through the thick windows of the apartment, she could see life gathering outside, attracted by the temporary breach. Black silhouettes fluttered in the nebulous green folds of the cloud-ocean: mothlike fliers, the size of a human hand, dangling improbably long legs; spherical membrane sacs, which would occasionally burst in a shower of purple ichor; and long, wispy, feather-snakes, lazily beating triplicate pairs of webbed wings.

"It's dangerous," she said.

"Polya, you must understand. If my Father finds out, he won't just take the lash to me. I've messed up too many times for that. They'll strip me of my name. I'll be destitute, sent off to grind nutrient paste in some orbital processing center."

"I can't imagine what that would be like, Excellency," said Polya, her face hard as crystal.

"I know what you were, Polya. Before the war. All that gear you've got in your head. The bioengineering. That's why I know you can do it." He lowered his voice to a conspiratorial whisper. "For what it's worth, I've always hated what we've done here. We talk about liberation and reunification, but our system's no better than yours. Anyone can see that."

She looked him up and down. He was serious. Her tactical centers were humming, processing this information. Polya reviewed her options. She could leave the kid to the fate he deserved, or take the risk for a big reward. And how big was the risk? She had given the planet plenty of chances to kill her before, and she was still here.

"I look forward to concluding this business with you, Master Partek."

⊕

Domestic equipment would be no good against a filter failure. Polya attached a canister of mineral-leaching agent to the distribution system on her back. She rigged up a high-heat auto-scrubber, a steelwool scourer on a tele-scopic flexi-shaft, and a broad-gauge chemspray, then tested all three. Just like her grandmother taught her: check your systems twice an hour until you're dead, then check them once an hour after that.

With the two drones projecting a containment field over the utility floor hatch, Polya lowered herself into the thick, rancid atmosphere of Monda. Her neck pulsed as her ambi-gland swelled, filtering toxins from her passageways and distributing aggressive countermeasures. Polya's caste were bred to fight in environments like these. A normal human would already be two-thirds dead.

The level was crawling with fetid life. Mossy growths and mold blossomed across the walls, beginning to devour the building. In one corner, bacteria had multiplied sufficiently to form mats, which respired with a slow, insistent pulse. The white shapes of silvercrabs darted and scattered over them.

Polya tweaked the chemical compound in her sprayer to a hydrocarbon, a cleaning oil, and adjusted the pressure so that it was expelled from the nozzle as a thin mist. Out of her belt pouch she took a firelighter, then pulled the trigger and lit up the mist, turning her sani-spray into a temporary flamethrower. The scuttling creatures and bacterial colonies wilted and deflated under the head of flame, and she swept their husks into the waste disposal unit at the center of the room.

The disposal unit itself was flecked with growths. It sagged beneath old food containers and rotten meal remains now being devoured by swarms of wriggling, worm-like creatures. There were some items of value amongst the waste—a few old clothes, a broken electronic device—now fully ruined by their exposure to the planet's life.

Something caught Polya's eye. She shifted the container to one side and stuck her hand into the piled waste. Her skin tingled as mites began to attach themselves. A hard, smooth object met her fingers. She clamped them shut and pulled it free.

It was an irregular crystal, between pink and purple, shining faintly from within as it caught the light. Glow. The addicts in the slum-quarter would chip shards from one like this and dissolve them in bitter tea. It was worth a lot, she guessed; five times as much as the boy was offering her. It was also highly illegal. She put it in her pocket.

As she stood, a wave of dizziness hit her, and the temperature in the room dropped. Her vision blurred and grew dark at the edges. A wedge of clay formed in her throat, dragging a net across her windpipe. Detecting a threatening spike in foreign toxins, her ambi-gland had gone into overdrive, restructuring her breathing passages and releasing its own hormones to mitigate the threat.

She had not noticed the white

growths on the wall. Now she looked closer and recognized what she had been too sloppy to see before. A tremble of instinctual terror ran through her body. It was a sight that Polya had been taught from birth to hate and fear. A colony of corpse-pale polyps, curling curiously from the wall. The Enemy was here.

They quivered on rubbery stalks, extending tiny tendrils into the atmosphere. As she approached, her gland contracted again. The fungus had sensed her interest, pumping the air with a visible mist of toxic spores. Her breathing dragged like a heavy chain through her body. All her tactical systems had shut down; she was operating on pure organics now.

The gland in Polya's neck throbbed. Her fingers ached, twitching sluggishly at the controls of her sprayer as she checked it. It wouldn't be long before she blacked out. She dragged the thick collar of her overalls over her mouth and doused the wall with an acrid burst. The cloying sensation in her head briefly relaxed before welling up again.

The fungal advance-growth of the Enemy was incredibly toxic; a worthy foe. Any normal human would already be undergoing digestion. But it had not counted on Polya na Labbardi, and now she was on the attack.

The polyps were fused cleanly to the wall, as if they were an off-growth of the structure itself. They struck back at every cloud of sanitizer with a pulse of toxins. Holding an arm across her face, she alternated volleys of biocide and flame with physical force, hacking and striking at the growths with the sharp edge of the auto-mop.

Her body screamed out, but behind her mask she was smiling. She had not tasted battle in so long, and it was longer still since she had tasted the only sweeter joy: to see one's enemy wilt and crumble under a storm of fury and flame.

⊕

Polya came back up through the hatch to Partek junior, his skin twitching in anxiety.

"You're my savior, Polya."

"It is my pleasure to serve," she said, meeting the boy's eyes, "for such generous compensation."

"Of course," said the boy, nodding. "You didn't find anything else down there?"

Polya considered the chunk of Glow in her pocket. It was a risk to handle it. She could sell it back to the boy for a price, maybe get him to double what he'd offered her. But until she'd seen the money, she didn't trust him. Better to keep several options open.

"Nothing but waste," she said.

"Ah, that's good," he said, sliding his tongue over his lips. "That's good."

From upstairs came the hydraulic hiss of shutters.

"They've arrived," whispered the boy.

⊕

Lord Barnival Partek's jaw grimly conveyed the unassailable authority of a senior Terran administrator. The starched white fabric of his uniform looked as thick as armor plating, a high collar wrapping his neck in a death grip. He was flanked by a gene-amped clone bodyguard; his wife was pouring a glass from one of the Terran wines Polya had salvaged.

"I am disappointed in you, son," said Lord Partek, "Although I cannot say that I am surprised."

His voice was pitched finely between disinterest and contempt. Lady Partek joined the attack.

"For your father to return, after a hard year on the Council working to protect this family, to rumors of unspeakable debauchery in his own home!"

Polya had done her best, but the boy hadn't been able to cover things up. Just as well she had held onto the Glow. Her payment was looking shaky.

Her Ladyship's face was the colour of fresh lava, matching the gleaming jewels on her chest. As she advanced, she took off her trim coat, lined at the collar with the skin of some unfortunate creature—a cousin of the rug downstairs—and threw it to the clone, who caught it one-handed, barely shifting its stance.

A tactical positioning module, Polya guessed. When she had entered the room, the simian quasi-human had changed position again, logging her as a new variable. No one else acknowledged her existence. She was glad of that, for now.

"Despite our investment in your upbringing, you treat us like this," continued Lady Partek. "Some of it might perhaps have been bearable. The orgies. Even the appropriation of your family's money to support your dissident lifestyle. But selling illegal substances to lowlifes out of our home. The Partek villa!"

The boy had his back against the wall.

"Account for yourself, son," pronounced his father. Polya felt a twang of sympathy. She knew what it was like to disappoint your family. She was fortunate that her own had not lived to see her undergo the curious version of mercy the Terrans afforded their enemies.

The boy looked from Lady Partek to

Lord Partek. Then he looked at Polya. She saw something shift in his features as their eyes met. He suddenly relaxed.

"Mother, I had not wanted to say anything. You know I have a sensitive nature. The truth is that I have been hiding something, but I can do so no longer, if only to protect my own honor."

His mother sneered. The boy turned to his father, searching for a more receptive audience.

"You've never approved of my sympathies for the natives, father..."

His parents' arms were folded, but neither interrupted. He continued. A tactical alert started pinging in Polya's head. This could be bad.

"The fact is that our maidservant has taken me into her confidence; out of sympathy for her circumstances, I had hidden some things from you. It is, I regret to say, she who has been dealing in these forbidden substances, and she has been using our home to do so. After all, you pay her so very little. I believe she is even carrying some on her person as we speak."

Polya searched for an indignant rebuttal. But the uncomfortable fact of the Glow crystal was jutting into her side.

All three Parteks now swivelled on her. She met the boy's eyes directly.

His face slowly twisted from panic into mocking and cruel satisfaction, and a century's worth of Monda's foulest curses died in her throat.

"Detain her, Claw," said Lord Partek. The clone advanced on her like an assault vehicle. There was nothing she could do.

◌

The storeroom was small and dark. At least it was clean – Polya had sanitized it two hours earlier. Not much she could do on the lock without tools. She rattled through the codices and doctrines saved to her tactical log. For the fifth time, she reached the end of her options, none of them offering a chance of success exceeding point-three percent.

Every warrior must make peace with their end. Mondanese soldiers could not look forward to a gentle exit from the world; theirs was a war that would never finish, and the weapons of the Enemy were neither swift nor precise. Perhaps it would be dissolution in a cloud of bio-acid, or perhaps their body would be devoured from within by a plague-swarm.

But Polya could not imagine an end more ignominious for the last issue of the House of Labbardi than this. She entertained an image of herself gouging her thumbs into the Partek boy's fat, wet eyes. But the fault had been her own. She had allowed herself to be deceived and tempted. No amount of money could do her any good now. Even if she escaped, she would have to get out of the city. Maybe even off-world. Her ancestors would go a long time without an offering.

There was a twinge in Polya's neck. A familiar, insistent cloying around her nose and mouth. A sudden urge to relax. Polya guessed what had happened. On the sleeve of her undershirt hung a thread of the white growth that she had exterminated in the lower level. She had fought in enough of the fungal wars to know that it had not got there by accident. In the fury of the battle, it sensed its defeat and identified the only escape route as her. Even in this quantity it could still easily overpower a human that didn't have Polya's defensive bio-mechanisms.

It had been a long time since Polya had felt she had any power over anything. Now, she held the existence of this sentient thing in her hand. She raised a fist to crush it into a milky smear.

But something pinged in her head; her hand stayed still. A new factor had been flagged. She logged the fungus into her options, recalling one of her grandmother's trademark doctrines: maximum adaptability, improvisation, and flexibility. But even Semna na Labbardi might have shied from the course of action Polya was considering.

Polya turned her attention to her breathing. It was a process she had been taught by the Spiritualists as a child: visualizing one's own lungs as the lungs of the city, and one's body as the great stalactite, a perfect system in its strength and balance. Her vision dimmed, and time slowed. The nodes and switches of her bio-digital anatomy presented themselves like a circuit. She practiced her control, artificially raising and lowering her pulse, deliberately secreting hormone bursts. Then, she raised the white strands to her face, and inhaled.

Red clouds flashed in front of her, her neck burned, and countermeasures surged through her body. Breath by breath, Polya suppressed her automatic responses. With each respiration, she felt the presence become clearer. She had felt it before; in the heat of battle it had been a nightmare that she had strained with her entire being to repulse. In the quiet and darkness of the storeroom, it was different. A vast network of beings, all sharing elements of a single sentience, unknowable, in a world without light or shadow.

She began to recognize something more familiar in it, something almost human. Aggression. Hunger. Fear. She and the Enemy circled each other warily.

Deep in myth, there were tales of warriors who had bridged their minds with the world-fungus; a suggestion that the relationship between the humans of Monda and their planet had not always been one of war. Caste doctrine had labeled these stories as lies and pacifist-ecologist agitprop. A soldier's instinct should be to respond with aggressive countermeasures as soon as it felt the first alien strands worm into their mind. Since the occupation, the stories had begun to spread again. Polya had heard whispers in the slum-quarters' alleys: the Mondanese may look like Terrans, but they really shared a soul with the other life of their planet.

She allowed the fungus to taste her emotions. It was no longer attacking, but exploring, probing at her. As a show of power, Polya briefly allowed the fungicides in her blood to surge again, and she felt the sentience retreat. Stabilizing, she began to set out her thoughts in clear and open sequence: an offer. A bargain. Co-operation, and mutual gain. Around each idea, the fungal entity closed its neural tendrils in investigation. She felt inquiry. Consideration.

Clearing her mind again, she presented the keystone of the proposition. A host in exchange for help. Her neck throbbed again as the fungus focused all its energy on this final concept. Then, it subsided, and her mind warmed. Understanding. Acceptance.

Polya respired deeply and allowed her countermeasures to surge to full capacity. The sentience in her mind winked out; the room came back into focus, and she vomited into the corner. Her clothes dripped and her skin fizzled. She'd need all her grandmother's blessings now.

①

"Water," Polya shouted.

She rapped at the door again, holding one eye to the crack. The Parteks had probably returned to familial bickering while they waited for the security squads to arrive. Perhaps they would simply dispose of her at their own convenience. The rights of indentured natives were a subjective matter on occupied Monda.

"I need water!"

A shadow moved in front of the door. From its movement and size, Polya could tell it was the clone. Better than no one coming at all, but only just.

"Please," she said, working desperation into her voice.

The clone was most likely a model without empathetic capabilities. It never hurt to try. For a second, the shape outside was still. Then it spoke, in a slurred, childish voice.

"Prisoner. Request. Water."

The shadow cleared, and Polya saw the neuro-lash at its waist as it walked away.

①

She attacked as soon as it entered, thrusting her wrist towards its face. The container of water hit the floor in a wet explosion of glass. The clone shifted, its huge body off-balance. Polya grabbed at it. She wasn't strong enough to bring it down neatly; its enormous weight knocked her backwards, a hand clamping around her right arm before she could squirm free.

Pushing her onto her knees, it grappled with her like a child with a doll. Her bones and muscles buckled. She tucked her head into her chest and held her left wrist to her body, denying the creature an opening. It grunted as it thrust an arm like a utility lifter's power claw around her neck. It was too strong. Her eyes blurred as it began to squeeze. She'd made a good fight of it—at least her ancestors would know that—but it was over.

She recalled the defense academy. The cadets had complained that hand-to-hand would be useless against fungus and bacteria. That hadn't stopped the bigger and stronger male cadets picking on her, the girl from a famous family. Her grandmother had shown no sympathy. "You have to learn the price of your name," she'd said. But, eventually, she'd shown Polya a few things.

Her eyes were growing dimmer, the clone's arm tightening around her neck. Polya tried to find the muscle memory, hidden under layers of organic and cybernetic wiring. Somewhere, she found it.

Polya pushed herself forward as hard as possible against the clone's arm. Feeling it pull back, she released completely and threw herself backwards, hooking a leg behind its knee. Unbalanced, the creature toppled, bringing her down on top of it. It still had a hold of her right arm, but her left was free. She lifted it, pulled back her sleeve, and wiped a full load of the fungal strands across its face. It rose, swiping at the mess with its arm, but it had already inhaled. Its hand went limp.

Her overalls were drenched with sweat. There was no time to rest. The clone was already starting to twitch slightly. She inspected its eyes; the tell-tale yellow flecks were forming in the sclera. Just like so many friends of hers in her lifetime of war.

①

A Mondanese warrior was trained to pick out the signs of fungal domination. Most people would be unable to distinguish it from the effects of a night on hard narcotics. The yellow in the eyes, the odd patterns of speech, the occasional stagger in the step. Walking behind the clone, Polya suppressed the urge to make a big hole in its head with the pistol she had taken from it. She had done the same to people she liked a lot more, as soon as she'd seen the head start to move in that way, the feet falling oddly and off-balance.

They surprised the family in the dining room, complexions undimmed from the earlier encounter. Polya guessed that parental discipline had evolved into marital dispute, with Lord and Lady at each other's faces and the boy cowering to one side.

Barnival Partek looked from Polya, to the gun she had leveled at his head, to the neuro-lash in the hands of his once-loyal henchman.

"Claw," he said, "Be a good boy. Put that thing down and come to boss."

The clone shook its head gently.

"He does what I say now," said Polya, "and so do you. Sit down."

It was a distinct pleasure to strip the pathetic honorifics and kowtowing from her speech.

They hesitated. She warmed up the pistol and fired a shot into the far wall, shattering several of the Terran ceramics that she had tidied earlier. Lord and Lady Partek sat.

"Here's what's going to happen. You're going to contact the port authority and commission a transport to pick you up from the dock at this level. Any questions, you tell them you forgot something on the orbital station. Anything other than that, and Mistress dies."

Partek looked dejected. He'd probably never been held hostage by his cleaner.

"You won't make it, you know."

"I've made it through worse. Let's go," said Polya.

She kept her weapon on his wife as Lord Partek trudged towards the door. Her operational modules had flooded her nervous system with combat stims, leaving her unable to think about anything except getting out of the city alive. That could be dangerous; she flipped a mental switch to lower the maximum threshold of the stim-dose.

Lord Partek gave the clone a strange wheedling look as he passed it, as if begging it to change sides again. Its face was utterly blank, although its eyes followed him across the room with precision. Maybe there was something of the old wiring left in there. Polya waved her fingers towards Lady Partek, beckoning her to move as well.

Something crashed behind Polya; in full combat readiness, she swiveled and lifted her weapon. Lord Partek had launched himself onto the clone, wrapping both hands around its neck and scrabbling in the direction of its command console. It was a brave attempt. Polya even felt a little sorry for the man when his former slave tossed him onto the floor like discarded clothing. She kept her weapon trained on him as he lay.

"Enough messing around," she said.

A buzzing hiss cleaved the air, and Lord Partek's head snapped to one side. The clone, face still impassive, had struck him with its neurolash. Polya held a hand up to it.

The lash sang out again, this time striking Lady Partek with a wet crack. Polya winced. Partek Junior began to frantically scramble away, but the clone's lash caught him mid-stride and knocked him off his feet.

"Stop!" said Polya to the clone, "This is not what we agreed."

It didn't respond. Again, it let the lash fly. Both older Parteks were rolling on the ground in agony; now the creature went in for the boy, striking him again and again. He struggled to hold his head upright, bubbles of blood and spittle at his lips and steaming red welts across his face. His mouth produced a string of incoherent sounds as the neuro-barbs on the lash scrambled his speech centers. Polya could imagine what he was trying to say.

"Stop," she said to the clone. Things hadn't gone to plan. Polya didn't need the situational alerts at the side of her vision to tell her that. The three Terrans were no good to her dead, and they were still humans. The soldier in Polya couldn't murder a prisoner in cold blood.

She made a decision—an imperfect one, guided by a surface-level appraisal of risks and benefits, and minimal tactical consideration. She lifted the pistol at the clone's misshapen skull.

"Stop," she said again. No reaction.

She pulled the trigger. But her hand didn't move.

Polya's fingertips flickered and burned. Momentarily, her breathing was interrupted; her stomach tied itself in knots. Shock and stress, she thought. Break through it. She willed her finger to go down over the trigger. It hovered. A black halo sprouted from the perimeter of her field of vision. The shouts and moans of the Partek family echoed dimly through her skull like a faulty recording.

It took Polya a second to realize what was happening. It took her a full three to realize how stupid she'd been. She'd let the world-fungus into her system, and taking its lack of resistance as evidence of her domination, she'd overestimated herself. Her attention had been on the high-proximity scenario while the fungus had been worming into her command structures, knocking out her defenses one by one, infiltrating every critical node.

Against her will, she lowered the gun. Her body started moving itself towards Barnival Partek, sprawled on his back like a wounded feathersnake. Polya's feet placed themselves in front of each other with brutal determination, as she strained everything to hold herself still. It was too late. She was putting out a level-five fire with a bucket of water and a mess-tin.

When she reached Partek, she took his head in her hand. He wriggled in her grasp, but she was strong. Stronger than she'd ever been. She felt something swell in her throat and saw Partek's eyes bulge in panic. Then she spewed a string of globules into his face. He made a few frantic swipes and fell limp.

The clone let the body of Lady Partek slump to the floor after doing the same to her. It met Polya's eyes with a glacial gaze.

"Clean," it said. The word didn't come from its mouth. It didn't come from the creature at all. It came from inside Polya, the same thing that was inside the clone, the same thing that was now inside the Parteks. It was not a word but a thought. It coalesced from a storm and etched itself on the core of her brain in a language beyond classification.

Clean. Wipe the stain away. Eliminate the impurity. Purge the toxins from the body. It was command and invocation, a divine force rising from within. It shone as clearly as a sun, a beacon to cut through Monda's swirling ocean of clouds.

Polya felt a sickness rising in her gut. This house disgusted her. These clumsy, improbably four-limbed creatures had gouged a hole in the rock and pumped it with heavy metals, twisted it into hideous angles. They sprayed it with chemicals that smothered all life, it was a waxy cell in which their progeny could bear out its life cycle. And this, she knew, was a poor suburb of the main colony, in which a million pale, wriggling creatures lived, all sucking the life from the world and then fighting one another for a share of the spoils.

The halo had disappeared from her vision now, and she saw more clearly than she had ever seen before. Her movements were no longer constrained.

She flexed her fingers in exploration.

The bodies of Lord and Lady Partek were standing now. She knew that they would also see the way. They were not others anymore, but part of one great organism, ageless and tireless, that had conquered the world eons ago.

She felt the strength of the great webs radiating across the world-roof, spanning kilometers, strands dancing in coordination. She heard the churning of nutrients in the farm nodes, where thick ropes of fungus hung, mycelia stretching into the fertile clouds of the sea to gather food.

She was not enslaved or coerced. She was free. But she was suffering from the deep and burning affliction of the sickness around her. There was no choice but to remove it.

She used the body that had been Lady Partek to open the command console and deactivate the filters of the house. No biosecurity alarm sounded. In their nostrils and lungs, they sensed the pure, delightful atmosphere of their own world, creeping into this place, reclaiming it. Across the world, they were advancing on this place. They would expunge the rot, and the world would once again be clean.

◑

DEEP CLEAN

=JOE ANDERSON=

DESERT MAN

DESIGN BY ALYSSA ALARCÓN SANTO, PHOTOS COURTESY OF THE SCHOALS FAMILY (CIRCA 1970s)

In 1956, the Hali Desert was as it is today: bare, lifeless, and utterly flat. The town that now stands at its edge and bears its name did not exist then as anything more than a few shacks inhabited by hermits and naturists who, for reasons of their own, chose to live as close as possible to what has been called the "Plain of Dust".

Halfway through the 144-mile drive down what was then known simply as the Hali Desert Road, Betty Nelson told her husband, Lou, to stop the car.

The young couple had been married the year before, and they were taking their first cross-country trip together to see Betty's family in California for Thanksgiving. It was late afternoon, the sun close to the horizon. While it never snowed in the Hali, the lateness of the season meant that it was cool, so the car windows were rolled up.

There was no radio reception that far into the desert, so, having nothing better to do, Betty pulled her compact from her purse and, for the sixth time in an hour, checked herself in the waning light.

Lou had been driving through the desert much of the day; first the Colorado, now the mountainless plain of the Hali. For hours their surroundings had been completely static, as though they were actually standing still, and the only thing really moving was the sun as it slowly traced its arc overhead. That's why, as she absently angled her mirror toward the horizon to catch some of the early evening's fading light, Betty could not immediately comprehend what she saw. After a moment, she clapped up the compact and spun around toward the window, looking slowly over every inch of the flat ground stretching off in the distance.

But Betty Nelson saw nothing. She turned away and sat straight in her seat. It was such a small thing that she must have imagined it. But as she looked back to the horizon, still seeing only the razor-straight horizon under the gloaming sky, she could not convince herself. After all, who would imagine seeing something so inconsequential, so nearly unnoticeable?

Betty opened her compact again and faced Lou, who drove on unawares. If the earth had not been so level, the road so straight, the ride so smooth, she wouldn't have found it again. She'd never have noticed it in the first place. It was no more than a speck in the mirror,

and in half-hearted disbelief she tried to scratch it off like a grit of dirt. But the small, twinkling spot remained.

"What's wrong, sugar?"

"I don't know." Betty answered absently. "Nothing."

"Well, what are you looking at?"

"I don't know." Betty said again after a moment, too distracted trying to figure the answer out for herself to have noticed Lou asking the question.

"Well, what's it look like?" Lou smiled, assuming she was playing some game he was not yet privy to.

"I don't know, Louis. Pull over." She looked in her mirror, then back to the horizon again, but said nothing more.

They drove on through the Hali and, eventually, into Indio, not speaking of the incident again until Lou brought it up a few nights later at Thanksgiving dinner. The whole table wondered out loud about what she might have seen, but Betty, red-faced, brushed it off as nothing. The Nelsons wouldn't speak of it again until years later, when, watching the news on the RCA ColorTrak television that Lou bought her for their 15th anniversary, Betty saw a report about an event called "Mirror Camp."

☽

Normally, a quiet desert—its sparse, picturesque landscapes under richly-clouded skies—is cathartic. But as I travelled back and forth along the length of the Hali portion of the I-10, I found it easy to understand why Betty might have thought she was seeing things. The plain of the Hali, a single, unbroken field of dry earth, borders the fading edge of Joshua Tree and stretches south and east, well beyond the Arizona line where vegetation and variety finally appear a few miles before the town of Cecina.

The desert is so flat, the highway—really just a widening of the old desert road—doesn't rise more than a few inches from the ground at any point. Even the wind barely seems to blow through the void. If not for the fact that the Hali is so empty—or, so expected to be empty—the Desert Man might never have been noticed at all.

INTERVIEW TRANSCRIPTION

INTERVIEWEE: Officer Ron Jerrington

NOTE: Pauses or transitions in dialogue such as "um" have not been included in the transcription. Additional observations by the interviewer have been denoted with brackets.

[BEGIN TRANSCRIPT 00:00:05]

RON JERRINGTON: Not that anything ever happened out there. Every once in a while, you'd get a drunk driver out on the edge close to town, but most days there wasn't even that.

But that one day.... It wasn't the worst thing I ever saw—it wasn't bad at all. I've seen some bad stuff. It wasn't that. It was just—I don't really know how to say it. It stuck with me.

> *[Officer Ron Jerrington was one of only a handful of Arizona State Troopers that regularly patrolled the desert road in the 1960s. There are even fewer officers that run the line today.]*

> *[He was sent out as part of a special initiative to break up the burgeoning drug trade along the western half of the border with Mexico.]*

RJ: I was always checking the weather report to see if it was going to be cool or a hot one. The one thing you wanted to make sure of was your water. Besides the fact that you could die if you didn't take in enough water, it got real easy to hallucinate.

If I hadn't heard about those reports—the experiments later on, the stuff with the mirrors—I'd never have said anything. But if I hadn't had any water that day, if there was so much as a chance that I'd just been seeing things, I'd probably have taken this story to my grave.

[It was almost noon and Jerrington was nearing the end of his four-hour workday. Shifts in the Hali were kept short due to the conditions.]

[00:00:57]

RJ: So, every time I went out, I took four canteens with me. Three would normally cover me for a shift, but that day it was especially hot out—those old uniforms made you sweat like crazy, too—and I was almost half-way through the fourth bottle and I was getting a little worried.

So, I'm sitting there on my motorcycle, just kind of thinking of how far away I was from everything, and I take my helmet off to get some fresh air on my head. I lean over, put it down on the ground next to the bike.

RJ: As I'm straightening up, in the rear-view mirror, I see the damnedest thing. This little twinkle that has no business being there. I move my head around just to make sure it's not an insect or a glob of something on the mirror, but that spot sticks right there. I can't help but think to myself, "What the hell can that be? Part of a plane broke off?"

I turn around, but I don't see anything. I turn back and look in the mirror again—there it is. So I get off my bike, cross the road, and look out into the distance.

[00:01:51]

[Officer Jerrington brings a liver-spotted hand over his heavy brow. Although the skin around his eyes is heavy and wrinkled with his 74 years, the look of searching astonishment—as though he's still trying to figure out the mystery of what he saw—is as clear as it must have been on the day he saw it.]

RJ: There was nothing.

[He holds his hand up in disbelief.]

RJ: So I go back to my motorcycle and check the mirror one more time, thinking it must be gone. But it's still there. It was the damnedest thing. What could it be that I could see it in the mirror and not straight-on?

RJ: Being a police officer, it was my duty to check out suspicious sorts of things like that. And, really, just being curious for my own self, I put my helmet back on, wheel my bike around, cross the road, and head out there.

I went out four, five miles, well away from the road, well away from anybody even having a chance of finding me if I wiped out or anything.

> *[Jerrington leans forward in his well-padded armchair, putting his elbows on his knees and his chin in his hand, still trying to make sense of it for himself even though the phenomena is now well-documented.]*

RJ: I don't know. Just nothing.

[END TRANSCRIPT 00:02:34]

The following is an excerpt from the diary of Dorothy-Anne Mullenberg, née Creely, age 13 at the time. It is reprinted from a copy received in the mail by the office of Dr. Paul Johnston, two weeks after Mirror Camp I.

The Big Family Trip, day 3. We drove through the desert all day today. Daddy was driving. I hate the desert. It's hot and it makes the car smell. Mama said that this family trip was going to be so much fun, but all we've seen so far is a few boring old ghost towns and every Bob's Steak Shack there is. Daddy loves Bob's Steak Shack, but I can't stand the smell. They all smell the same, like my brother when he comes in after football practice. Francis is here too, and that doesn't make it any better. From the way he acts, you wouldn't think he was actually older than me. He can't stop pestering me. I tell him that he's being immature, but he never listens.

Today, he was wearing a stupid pair of sunglasses and telling me they were spy glasses. I asked him how they were spy glasses and he said he could see what was behind him. "What's there to see?" I asked. "There's just a lot of desert." He said he could see a tree out there, and I told him that was silly. There wasn't a tree out there. There wasn't anything out there. But he kept saying there was something, and maybe it must be a tree. I was looking right at him, though, seeing everything he saw behind him, and I didn't see any tree. I didn't see anything at all.

So then he turned around and looked out the window for a long time. Then he looked back at me for a while, kind of funny, like maybe he was looking through the mirrors in his glasses again. Then he took them off and didn't say anything at all for a while. I almost picked them up to look myself, but it's not mature to play with toys.

Bobbi Johnston is the wife of Dr. Paul Johnston.

"I'm the wife of the man who made the Desert Man."

She speaks with an earnest, good-natured smile. Their sunny kitchen, with a large window over the sink that looks out on a colorful spring garden, is a far cry from the Cecina Tech laboratory where I'd interviewed her husband the day before.

"Did he wear his jacket for you?"

"He never wears that thing, but we had a whole conversation yesterday morning on whether or not he should wear it when he saw you. I told him not to, that he looked fine as he was. Not wearing it just seems more, you know, authentic.

'The wife of the man who made the Desert Man.' That's not really accurate, of course. Except that I'm his wife."

She breaks into a fit of giggles and I find myself laughing along with her.

"You know, at first I thought it was just a ploy to get me alone for a few hours. This was before we moved in together. We'd been going out over a year by then, and one day he came to my dorm and said he was going for a trip into the desert."

"He said a friend of his had read an article or heard something on the radio about this thing that you could only see in a mirror and he wanted to check it out. He asked me if I wanted to come and I figured that it'd just be the two of us out there."

She puts her coffee cup down on a bright ceramic coaster and lays her hand flat on the table, giving a look as though she's about to dish out the town gossip.

"What I got was six physics geeks in a microbus, each waving around his own dollar-store compact mirror."

She laughs warmly at this, rocking a little in her chair, and I can't help but think that she'd tell the exact same story in the exact same way if her husband were sitting at the table with us.

Her laugh ends with a sigh and another sip of coffee.

"Paul is a wonderful scientist. Not a great activity planner."

I think about the pictures hanging on the walls of their home as I walked in.

Pictures of the family—Paul, Bobbi, and their two kids, a boy and a girl. Smiling in front of Big Ben and The Hoover Dam.

Another with just their son, very young, and Bobbi very pregnant, at Disneyland. They're all wearing Mickey Mouse ears.

"They wanted to take pictures, but, between the six of them, only one remembered to bring a camera. And he only had one half-used roll of film. No tripod or anything, either.

So, for the first few pictures, Paul or Jeff or Pete or someone would hold the mirror in one hand and try to take a picture with the camera in their other hand."

She holds a hand out in front of her, grasping an imaginary mirror, as she brings the other close to her face.

"They did that for a while, then decided that one person would hold the camera while someone else held the mirror. And then of course—and this was the best part—I said,

'Well, what if you're shaky?'

Now, I expect that they'll do the smart thing and put the camera on the roof of the van or something. But no.

Instead, one guy gets down on his knees, holds the camera over his head with both hands, and two other guys come along either side to steady him, like a human tripod."

"Two other guys get on their knees a few feet away and, together, hold up one of the compact mirrors while Paul snaps the picture."

She wipes her tearing eyes as she talks.

"I wish I'd had a camera because that's still the funniest thing I've ever seen!"

I give her a minute to take a breath and ask,

"What about the pictures?"

She strikes me as the sort of woman that, if there had been pictures, she'd have had them ready when I'd walked in.

"Well, that's kind of the tragic part of it, though it's not surprising.

A few days later, I went to the Fotomat to pick up the prints. Like I said, the first half of the roll had already been used up. When I opened the envelope I noticed that the first few pictures of—I don't know, maybe it was a party—were all blurry in a weird way, like the camera was broken.

I got this terrible feeling as I kept flipping though and, sure enough, every one of those pictures from the trip had the same problem.

Totally out of focus, every one."

It may have been tragic to Bobbi and Paul and the others, but a lot more pictures have been taken of that little speck on the horizon, and even the clearest of those taken before the first Mirror Camp show very little detail; the average composition includes the ground and the sky, bifurcated by the horizon, and a small, dusky spot in the far distance, just at the vanishing point.

UCSD researcher and Desert Man hobbyist Gordon Dunst notes that even finding where the Desert Man should be is an impossibility:

> **GD:** It would be easy to find where it should be if it didn't move. Which is to say that, in a way, it doesn't move, but in a way it does.

The interview is being conducted via internet voice-chat; Dunst is in Vienna for a scientific conference.

GD: It doesn't move in relation to the viewer; from the viewer's perspective it's always to the west, right at the horizon—about three miles. But if you're out there in the desert and you move three miles toward it or away from it, it's always still on the horizon, always three miles distant.

He begins an elaborate explanation of what the Desert Man might be, but the connection starts to break up and, soon, it drops out entirely. We're eventually reconnected, but he's late for a panel discussion and can only provide me with the two-minute version:

GD: Even though it's bizarre that this phenomenon's spatial placement is relative to the viewer, it's at least consistent. It's not like it moves around on its own or anything. We can't really explain the phenomenon, but we know it's playing by a certain set of rules and that it's not cheating.

While it may not be cheating, it does have a big home-court advantage. Desert climates are arid, yet measurable amounts of rain do occur in most deserts. But, as in so many things, the Plain of Dust is unique.

GD: Almost any desert is going to have water of some kind—in the air, deep in the ground, something—and where there's water, there's life.

Geothermal biologist Sandy Weisencamp is the curator at the National Desert Museum in Death Valley.

SW: What makes the Hali unique—kinda freaky, actually—is that there's just no water.

Annual rainfall measures in the tenths-of-millimeters, and when you get into those kinds of numbers, it's really just a guess. We're talking about a single, brief shower that's so light the sand just sucks it up. Once it's over, it's like it never happened.

There are still plenty of people who think it's some kind of mirage or mass-hallucination. The problem with the first theory is that a mirage can be seen straight on, but this can't.

And, of course, the problem with the second is: How do you photograph a hallucination?"

"It wasn't actually called 'Mirror Camp' then. We didn't have a name for it."

Dr. Paul Johnston has invited me to interview him in his lab at Cecina Tech. He is unassuming and quiet as he greets me, but as soon as I mention the big event, he's ready to start talking.

"The whole reason we made a big spectacle of it in the first place was because the science department needed the money. It was the late 70s; we were still feeling the effects of the oil crisis out here and some of the science and agriculture programs were about to get put on the chopping block. So it seemed like a no-brainer.

"The spot—they called it 'the spot' back then—had been talked about around town for a while by that point, so we just picked a Saturday, put some fliers up, and got our stuff together."

It was two years after the microbus trip and, by this time, Bobbi and Paul were married, with their first child on the way. Paul had graduated from Cecina Tech

and was working as an adjunct science instructor at his alma mater.

"I have to admit, it was for me and Bobbi and the baby as much as the school. I figured that, if we raised a little money, maybe I could get a full-time position here. Bobbi and some of her friends at the print shop took care of getting the word out while a few of us in the department brainstormed over what we'd actually do when we got out there.

"I don't remember who came up with the idea for a big mirror. It sounded like a good idea at the time. We knew we'd need to get the mirror off the ground so that everyone could see it, so we built a stage.

"It was really just a bunch of old folding tables and some plywood laid across the top. Took about ten minutes to set up. I'm amazed the whole thing didn't cave in, given all the people that ended up running across it. And getting that mirror. Now, that was a problem."

I ask Paul if he has any pictures of the original set-up. He looks around and pulls one off the wall behind me.

"I don't even know how this got here. I think Bobbi put it up."

He hands me the picture: framed black and white, looking out on the crowd from the rear, as though the photographer might be standing on the back of a truck. The stage isn't visible, but the mirror is. I hold the picture in my hands and he reaches over and taps on the mirror.

"That was the real pain in the butt. I thought somebody else was supposed to get it, other people thought I was supposed to get it, and without it, you were nowhere. So, I had to wing it."

The mirror in the picture is huge, at least 12 feet wide by five feet tall. Yet it would turn out to be one of the smallest mirrors that any camp event has ever featured.

"It wasn't actually a mirror—as in it wasn't a piece of glass backed with a silver solution. It was polished aluminum.

They were renovating the arts center at the time—renovating the lobby, even though the school was so strapped for cash. The morning of, I didn't have anything.

"I'd gone to a few places—shops, thrift stores—but there was nothing big enough. I didn't even know where to start. Walking around the campus, I see these big sheets of aluminum just sitting out on the sidewalk in front of the arts center."

He pauses for a moment, perhaps out of regret, perhaps out of pride.

"I had the truck," he stares at me, unblinking, "so I stole one."

The afternoon of the event, with the stage set up, the "mirror" was unveiled.

"It was propped up on this kind of patchwork series of easels. We didn't want to poke holes in it or anything because I had to take it back. So we did the best we could. We had this big sheet over it and my wife and I went up together and pulled the sheet off, and right away people started taking pictures."

"I can't imagine how many of them actually came out. So many people were right in front of the mirror and half of them were using their flashes, so I imagine some of them just got pictures of their own lights. But then someone pulled out a zoom lens and got up on stage, really close. And as he was snapping his pictures, he was shouting out to everyone that he could see something. Like... it wasn't just a spot.

"Word spread through the crowd pretty quick, and a few other people with zoom lenses came up on stage and started taking pictures too. Like I said, I was worried the whole thing was going to collapse. I'd have guessed it could hold the weight of maybe six people, and there were three or four times that many up on it. Then, with all this going on, some girl made a beeline for town and returned with a telescope."

He pauses for a moment. Finally, I ask. "Then what?"

"Well, she got up on stage and set up the telescope. She held it steady and pointed the lens of her camera into the eyepiece. She snapped a picture, looked into the telescope—I guess to make sure it was still aimed—snapped another picture, checked again, and so on. She took about a dozen shots that way.

"When she finished, she straightened up, looked over at me, and said, 'I can see him'. She said it right to me, and I remember thinking that it was funny she said 'him' and not 'it.' And then, of course, everyone started asking if they could look through the telescope, but she let me and Bobbi look first."

"What did you see?"

Paul adjusts his glasses. Much of the world decided the Desert Man wasn't a hoax a long time ago. Paul looks as though he's still struggling with it.

"It was a person, like she said. It looked like a man in a long, light-colored coat, with a hood."

"And that's it?"

"Yeah. Well, he's facing away. And—"

Another pause.

"And what?"

Paul looks at me and I can't help but think for a moment of Galileo, forced to deny his own knowledge. I wonder if that's how Paul feels now, as I face him with a question I already know the answer to.

"And he was holding a mirror. He was looking at us through it."

☽

The piece of aluminum Paul and Bobbi used for the first Mirror Camp was returned immediately after the event, completely unharmed. Paul even confessed what he had done to school officials, but the money he'd raised offset any hard consequences. It had to be officially acknowledged that a theft had occurred, but Paul was pardoned by the president of the college, who also wrote a letter of recommendation which helped Paul get hired on full-time the next spring.

That first Mirror Camp took place over the course of an afternoon. Mirror Camp 2020 is a three-day-long outdoor convention. There is, of course, a spike in the number of heat-stroke victims that report to Cecina-area hospitals during the event, and there have been a small number of deaths over the course of the previous camps. But the size of the crowd has only increased over the years. That's why Paul Johnston calls me in my motel room on the first day of this year's camp. It's 7 A.M.

"I can't do it. I'm sorry, it's just too much."

Paul has been back out to the Cecina Desert dozens, perhaps hundreds of times to study the phenomena, but never again like the first Mirror Camp. Never with such a setup, never with so much company. Neither he nor Bobbi have been to Mirror Camp for at least 35 years.

"All those people. In a lab—even in the field, usually—it's just you and the subject. You can block out the distractions pretty easily. If I were a sociologist, if I was there to study *them* instead of *it*, I'd be in heaven. But I'm not a sociologist."

I ask him if the costumes have anything to do with it.

"Well, yeah. I'm not a sociologist and most of them aren't really scientists. I mean, some of them are out there for a legitimate scientific interest, but most of them that go out there, they do it for something else.

"When we did that first set-up, we expected that everyone who was going to be there was going to be there for the science aspect of it. Now, it's like they're all coming out to dress up and party."

DESERT MAN

*The day that I first interviewed Paul, we ended
up on the phone with Bobbi and the two agreed to
go out and take a look at this year's camp. Bobbi
mentioned that he would be treated like a celebrity,
but Paul seemed hesitant. A few days later, during
the early morning phone call to my hotel room, he
tells me why he's changed his mind.*

"We were just watching the news. It doesn't
officially start until noon, and they're already
out there. Thousands of them."

Although the original event was closer to the center of the desert, over the years the meeting place has been moving farther and farther east, closer to Cecina.

The stage, too, is bigger. Not nearly big enough to hold all the cameras and scopes and all the people that hope to make it up there, but enough for a few dozen. And with organizers charging $20 for each device set up on-stage and $10 within a roped-off area extending about 100 feet out, it more than makes up for the expenses of putting on the relatively simple event. The school gave up Mirror Camp to private organizers ten years ago, but the science department still gets a charitable donation from the profits. Of course, there are scores more who set up their own gear outside of the stage area. There are even some entrepreneurs who charge fellow campers for using smaller versions of the mirror stage, such as standing atop camper vans.

Toward one end of the ever-lengthening line of cars and people, telescopes, cameras, and mirrors, I watch a young kid position a pick-up truck with an upright mirror strapped into the bed. A girl, thin and pig-tailed, maybe 15 years old, is directing him from the side. Another camper yells at her as she wanders into his shot and she skitters a little, then edges closer to the truck and keeps waving the boy into position. The mirror in the back of the truck is framed by thick woodwork with small shelves on either side, something from an old bedroom set. By the style, it might be older than Mirror Camp itself.

Once the boy, who introduces himself as Jay, has finished with the truck, he passes the keys to Daisy, his sister. She unlocks the gate and pulls half a dozen milk crates and wide wooden planks out of the bed and onto the dusty ground. Sensing that I'm about to ask, Jay flatly says, "Yeah. Our mom had a thing for *The Great Gatsby*."

As she's setting up the crates and planks, Daisy explains, "These are for people to stand on or put their cameras on. We lost money last year because the side of the truck was too high for short people. I don't know why, but there are a lot of short people that come to this."

As it is, the bottom half of the mirror is mostly covered by the side of the bed. I ask them why they don't reposition the truck, open the tailgate, and set the mirror on the open gate, facing toward the Desert Man. They stare at each other for a moment before Daisy tosses the keys back to her brother and walks back out to direct him.

⏀

Paul was right. There is something about the current batch of attendees that is markedly different from those who came to the first Mirror Camp. The Desert Man has become a pop culture phenomenon of sorts, making the event look more like a Star Trek convention than a collection of science enthusiasts. Of the thousands sweating out in the hot sun, at least a third are wearing some approximation of the same uniform; a long, hooded coat or cloak, of a light brown or yellow color.

"Some people have said he's pale. But it's hard to be sure, since he's facing away and all you can see in his little hand mirror are his eyes. Some people put on white face paint, but I'd just sweat it all off."

Donna Abramowitz chuckles, happy enough in her yellow hoodie under an old, faded trenchcoat. She is 45, about five feet tall, and she says she's been coming to Mirror Camp for ten years.

"I went to my first few camps and it was just so fascinating, looking at him out there. I didn't have anything the first time—just a little compact mirror—but I chatted someone up and they let me take a look through their scope. It was actually a plugged-up rifle with a mirror mounted on the front. The guy had it on a tripod, like a camera."

She holds her hands up, as though holding a large gun. "It wasn't very powerful and the mirror was pretty dirty, but I could make out the shape of him, you know? I could see he wasn't just a dot. I came the next year and the year after that, and I eventually just realized that I wanted to be close to all this."

Donna owned a catering business in Nebraska. Now she works as a receptionist for a local doctor. "I tried getting the business back off the ground, but there just wasn't a market for it here." She turns to the side and holds her hands open, as though to embrace the entire crowd. "But I'm here! This is it! My apartment is, like, 40 minutes away and I can come out here any time I want."

I ask her if she ever does come out, besides during Mirror Camp.

"Oh yeah, all the time. A lot more in the fall, though, when it's cooler. Sometimes, I'll bring a tent." She looks out wistfully at the horizon, as though she can see that dark speck with her naked eye, straight on. "Sometimes I'll come out and spend the night with him."

The Desert Man has never moved. In every film and photograph, it's always in the exact same pose, and even the folds and creases of its coat are the same now as they were when the first pictures were taken. It looks like a man, but it must be some kind of statue. Mustn't it?

This steadfastness is only one of the puzzles surrounding the Desert Man, but it's one that two college students from Florida are taking advantage of.

Two days after this year's Mirror Camp closes, I'm driving my rental car to Palm Springs, where I'll catch a flight back home the next day. My route takes me back through the Cecina Desert. It's late in the day when I set out and the sun has just slipped under the horizon as I pass a van sitting close to the road.

Next to it, two young people are setting up gear. I probably wouldn't have stopped, but the girl, who is checking the batteries on a pair of walkie-talkies while the boy sets up a tripod, is wearing a black ballet leotard. I pull over.

Riq Dominguez is 21, Rachel Spitzer is 20. They're students from the University of Miami who decided to use their semester break to take pictures of the Desert Man. But these pictures are something new. In my research for this story, I've never come across anything like what they are about to do.

I introduce myself, tell them about the story I'm working on, and offer to help them get set up. Riq's tripod and camera seem pretty normal, except for the arm extension off the tripod that looks as though it was built just for the purpose of mounting the mirror. He pulls a zoom lens out of a photo bag; it's so big, he needs to hold it with both hands.

"I want to make sure I can get the highest detail possible."

It doesn't look like the sort of thing a student could afford. "The school photolab lent it to me."

He flashes the sort of smile that makes me wonder if the photolab knew they had lent it out.

Nearby, Rachel turns over the engine and sets out into the desert. Riq calls after her: "Don't forget to reset the trip meter." Rachel waves a hand out the window.

Riq looks into the distance through a pair of large binoculars. After a few minutes, the van is barely visible, but it doesn't get any smaller. A voice crackles over the walkie-talkie. "I'm here."

"Looks good," Riq responds. "See anybody?"

"Not a soul." He turns his head to address me, although his eyes stay fixed on the van, "If he's actually on the horizon line, like everybody says, from where we're standing now she should be right on top of him."

Rachel is a dot, close to the van but moving away from it. Soon, her voice comes over the walkie-talkie again. "Am I far enough away from the van?"

Riq turns to the LCD screen on the rear of the camera, holding a hand over it to cut the glare that still streams out over the horizon. "Yeah. Now just hold tight. I have to get everything adjusted."

He moves the tripod a few feet to the right, looks at the screen again, and begins adjusting the mirror. The adjustments become more and more subtle, until, finally, he taps the mirror very lightly, checking the monitor each time, until the alignment is perfect.

He calls her over the walkie-talkie again as he stares into the monitor. "I'm all set up. Stand up and walk a few feet to your left. Okay, now just put your arm out. Okay, bring it down about three inches and take two steps forward. Small steps."

"How's that?"

"Hold on." He taps the mirror again then looks back to his screen. "Okay, I think that got it. Go ahead and take your pose. Just make sure you stay in place."

Suddenly, he clicks off more than a dozen pictures, rapid-fire. He scrolls through the shots briefly, then calls on the walkie-talkie. "We got it. It's great. Come on back."

"Great."

Riq calls me over, but I'm momentarily distracted by the sky over the dimming horizon line. It is a color between red and gold. He calls again. "You want to take a look at these?"

I walk over and look into the small monitor on the camera.

Riq holds a hand up against the glare. In the frame, just off-center, is the Desert Man, faced away, hand up to hold his mirror. But now, next to him, is a beautiful girl in a dancer's pose. She's bent forward gracefully, one leg curled into the air behind her. A searching, wanting, adoring hand is held up to his, so that in the silhouette of the sunset, their hands embrace the mirror and one another in an impossible dance.

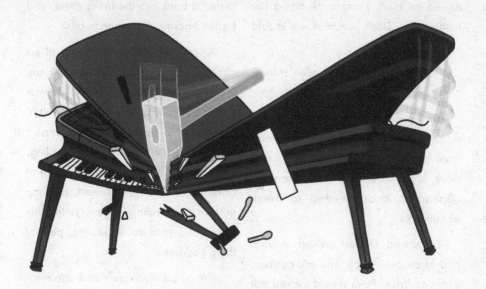

⇒SAM REBELEIN⇐
HECTOR BRIM
ILLUSTRATIONS BY ALYSSA ALARCÓN SANTO

When she'd been gone for seven days, Gil took an ax to her piano.

There'd been a small reception in his apartment after the funeral. Just Natalie's parents, his mother, a handful of friends, and a few neighbors, including Mrs. Preston down the hall. Gil did nothing the entire time but wish them all gone. They had no comfort to give. No reassurances of higher meaning or better places, which they did not believe in. That wasn't the kind of crowd they were, so it wasn't the kind of crowd Gil needed.

Mrs. Preston was the only exception. She'd once spoken to him in the elevator, convincingly and unsolicited, about reincarnated pets and the spirit realm. But Gil squirmed in her company. Even her words of sympathy and reassurances felt small and cold. She seemed to sense this, leaving the reception early, patting his arm, and telling him, "Knock on my door if anything comes up."

There was something ominous about it, like she knew something. It made Gil squirm even more. He finally managed to usher everyone out, and as the door closed on Nat's parents, he heard her mother say, "Don't you think we should stay a bit longer?"

"No," her father said, gentle. "Honey, come on. He wants to be left alone."

The door shut on that. *Alone* vibrated throughout the apartment. For a long time, Gil didn't move. He just stood there, black-suited and formal, leaning against the door, needing to break something.

He turned. Gazed around at what had been their home. The tall ceilings, exposed brick. Paint they'd picked out together. Shelves filled with their books and photographs. And in the corner, those bone-and-black keys she'd hunched over with her long fingers, smiling as she played him the songs she wrote privately on lunch breaks.

"You could be a famous singer," he'd told her once.

"But then I wouldn't sing for *you*."

The ax was buried in the hallway closet. Why he'd brought it with him when they'd moved down to the city, he couldn't say. Maybe a part of him knew.

He loosened his tie. Rolled up his sleeves. Tore the closet door open. He knelt, began tossing old jackets over his shoulder. A tennis racket. Cob-webbed shoes. He dug the ax out of the dust, hefted it back into the living room, and began hacking that piano to bits.

A long sliver of wood sliced at his cheek as pieces flew through the air. He felt the sting, but his whole life was sting now anyway, so what did it matter. He started with the keys, then moved sideways to the body. The jangling, springy chorus of snapping wires beat against his ears. He grinned, reveling in it. In the breakage of everything this once solid, formidable, smiling, perfect thing had been.

The ax crashed again and again.

Suddenly, a wire whipped across Gil's bicep and he stopped. Stood panting above the wooden ruin, debris scattered across the floor. The ax hummed, frozen above his head. He felt himself pulse. Felt the leak down his arm, on his cheek.

The way the truck had hit her as she stepped unknowing off the curb, her arm had nearly cracked in half. Right along the bicep, right *there*. Feeling the wire now across that same spot, on his own arm, he was right back there. Holding her as she went. Watching her arm twitch. Watching those long fingers go limp. The truck driver standing in the street, rocking back and forth on his heels. Retching. Weeping. Gil never heard his apologies. He just watched the arm twitch....

A sound. Soft and far-off. A kind of skittering slowly filling the apartment. Gil let the ax drop and clatter down out of his hand. He listened. Hundreds of insects, or tiny paws, scratching at the floor. Scrabbling across the wooden boards. A hollow, frantic scramble.

Gil frowned. Cocked his head. The noise grew louder. Louder. Began to roar throughout the room. But he couldn't tell what it was.

Someone was standing behind him.

He turned. He was alone. *Alone.* Of course he was. She was gone. But for a second, he'd *felt* someone. Felt a pocket of displaced air or... something. He couldn't explain it. He just felt watched.

The roar drowned this feeling out. His pulse, the leaks across his skin, quickened. He realized the noise was now joined by the coppery snaking whir of springs bouncing against each other. Gil turned again, looking around the room, starting to itch and sweat. What the hell was it? It sounded half-wooden, half... ivory. Sliding across the....

"Oh."

He looked down.

The debris of the piano was moving.

As he watched, it rolled itself across the floor and, slow but steady, wove itself into a wide, crooked heart.

Gil blinked at it. Then he threw up.

Because it wasn't really the crowd Gil belonged to, he didn't know what to do with... this. He didn't have the tools to process this kind of thing. And he knew, no matter how it sounded, that that was probably why his wife had waited an entire week to be known like this. Or felt, or whatever. Nat knew— she *must*—that she'd have to wait for a break. A moment when he'd actually listen, or see. Some kind of rock bottom. Watching him hack at her piano with an ax was probably the best chance she'd get. Like Gil, she'd been kind of a skeptic, so he *knew* she'd think like that. That is, *if.* If she really were....

Gil sat on the couch, knees tucked tight under his chin. He stared at the floor, at the wet spot from the puke he'd mopped up, right in the center of the piano heart. He'd carefully left the heart untouched.

He dug the heels of his hands into his eyes. Shook his head. Laughed. Tried to pull himself together. Laughed again. Gave up. He figured whatever was happening, he might as well go all in. And if he was starting to go crazy, what the hell. He cleared his throat. Looked around the room, feeling self-conscious. "Alright," he said. "Are..." He cleared his throat again. "Are you... here?"

There was a green and yellow light fixture in the hall. Something Natalie had brought down to the city, and loved.

It flickered on.

Gil began to cry.

A low rushing breathed down the hall. Gil held his breath. Sliding along the floor, around the corner, came a box of Kleenex. It slid to a halt just before the couch.

"Oh," he said.

☻

By sunset, he'd cried everything out. He sat calm on the couch, knees still tight against himself. Sore now, after sitting folded like that for hours. Clutching a wad of sodden tissues, he peered down the hall to the light fixture. Not sure what else to do, he said, just sort of confirming, "You're really here."

The light blinked.

Heat flooded his chest. "I... I miss you."

The light flickered.

Gil sat up. He stretched his legs and his knees cracked. He wrung his hands, thinking. "Are you... *mad* that I broke your piano?"

The light said nothing.

Gil nodded. "Okay." He sniffed, ran a hand under his nose. "Okay."

He figured out quick that he could ask Nat simple yes or no questions through the light. She'd blink once for yes, stay off for no. As long as he kept the questions simple, she could answer.

Over the next three weeks, every chance he got, he'd speak with her. And of course, told no one about it. Sometimes, she would float old pictures around to make him smile, or throw her jewelry across the room. Once, he'd felt a hand on his back. It made him jump and scream. But the hand wrapped around his shoulder, warm and safe. He melted into its company.

He sat under the hall light for hours every day. Talking, reminiscing, sometimes just staring. Silent. Trying not to hurt.

Finally, he worked up the strength to ask the most terrifying question he could think of.

"Are you in pain?" Gil sat slumped against the wall. He stared up at the light.

Waited for it to respond.

It didn't.

"Hey. Are you in *pain?*"

The light flickered. Wavering enough so that he wasn't sure.

"Are you in pain?" Through tears this time.

Another flicker.

"Hey. Are you *okay?*"

Nothing.

She wasn't sure. He could feel it. Could feel it through the walls. Some kind of aching uncertainty. A looseness or unbalance. Something... off.

It was after another week of this, of asking and crying and clinging to her, of barely leaving his apartment just to be *near* her, even if it was just a flicker and an echo of who she was, that Gil finally decided she probably needed help.

Something echoed through his brain: *Knock on my door if anything comes up.* Well. Something had definitely come up.

🕐

Even if she hadn't offered, Gil probably would have trusted Mrs. Preston more than any of his skeptic pals. Especially now that he'd isolated himself for weeks, barely answering their texts and calls. He and Mrs. Preston weren't friends. Not by any stretch of

anything. They said hello to each other when they crossed paths in the lobby. In the elevator sometimes, they chatted politely about the weather, city life, reincarnated pets that one time, spirits rarely, and... well, they *had* chatted about Nat. Or with her, even, when she'd been there.

That hurt to think about.

Mrs. Preston was maybe 80, a good 50 years older than Gil. He couldn't say what she did for a living, really, or call her voice to mind unless he thought hard about it for several seconds. She was just some (and he felt bad thinking this) generic, squat, sweet old lady in his mind. And he was pretty sure (and this made him feel slightly better) that to her, he was just some generic, tall young guy. But if anyone would believe in ghosts speaking through light bulbs and piano shards, he felt like it'd be her. Her door stank of sage and mystery every time he walked by it. She had that... vibe. A weird energy of *knowing* things. And at the reception, it'd seemed like she'd definitely known. Or guessed.

So.

He stood in the outer hall, peering down it at Mrs. Preston's front door. He worked his hands into his pockets. He glanced back at his own door, which felt like looking at Nat herself, now that she seemed to be in the very beams of his apartment. He looked away. Twisted his hands back and forth in his pockets. Dug his cheek into his shoulder, itching the old scab from the piano shard.

What exactly was he going to say to her? How *precisely* did he think she could help him? How could Mrs. Preston help Nat, furthermore? Did she need to "move on," whatever that meant? What if Mrs. Preston thought he was crazy? What if he... What if he *was*?

He shook those thoughts away. Useless at this point. He was too far in.

He stood there in the outer hall. His hands twisted harder. Faster. The cheek scab itched. With each second, the hallway grew longer.

"Fuck it," he muttered, and marched down the hall.

🕐

The whole thing came tumbling out in jagged starts and stops, almost as soon as Mrs. Preston opened the door. Gil stammered his way through the explanation of the piano and the light. He skipped over some parts that seemed more insane than others. But he was also describing his wife's ghost inhabiting his apartment, so what sounded insane versus what didn't felt like kind of a toss-up. The more Gil talked, the more self-conscious he felt. As he spoke, his hands never left his pockets.

Mrs. Preston listened to the whole thing, face twitching between confusion, concern, and something else.

"And I feel," he finished, at last, "that she's just... spaced out. Stretched. That her... I don't know, the spirit? Has just expanded into the whole place. Instead of being *in* her. And... well...."

He stopped. Something he'd said had made Mrs. Preston's eyes light up. They danced over him. He wasn't sure how to take that. Almost backed away from her.

She knew, he decided.

"It's funny you use that word," she said. "Expanded."

Gil shrugged. "It's how I feel. Or—"

"You think it's how *she* feels?"

"Of course," he said. "And, and confused. Lost. I know her, I can *feel* it." The words were more high-pitched, more desperate than he expected. His cheeks burned. *What am I saying?*

But Mrs. Preston just nodded, grinning wide.

"One moment," she said.

She shuffled away into her apartment, leaving the door open. Gil stood there. His mind railed at him. Called him stupid, told him to go back to his cage and hide with the dead. What the fuck did he think he was doing here? Bothering an old, kind woman with his bullshit.

He was just about to stalk shamefully back down the hall when Mrs. Preston returned, still grinning. She held her hands tight to her chest. Whatever she was holding, Gil couldn't see it.

She leaned against the jamb, sighed, and closed her eyes for a moment. Ran her thumbs in circles round the thing within her hands.

"My husband," she started. Stopped. Swallowed some sharp stab of tears. She tried again, voice stronger. "My husband. When he died, I didn't know what to do with myself."

Mr. Preston was a somewhat nebulous entity to Gil. From what he'd gathered, the man had died about two years before Gil and Nat moved in. She'd mentioned him once or twice, but only in passing.

Gil stood a little straighter, alert.

"Apparently," she continued, "he didn't know what to do either. Because he never left."

The bottom of Gil's stomach opened.

"I never knew," he said.

"Oh, yes," said Mrs. Preston. "His spirit was still with me. And in such pain.

I knew *I* wasn't ready to move on. But I could feel *he* wasn't ready, either. Because of me. I could feel it through the walls. And whenever he made himself known, whether it was just a little sign or a feeling I got, I could tell that he was still there because he was worried I wouldn't be okay alone."

Gil's eyes flicked down to her hands.

"We were both hurting," she went on. "But then a friend gave me this."

Her fingers blossomed and held out the thing she'd been hiding. A business card. She held it out to him, delicate, in both hands. To be offered, so ceremoniously, something so simple and secular, made Gil suddenly uneasy. He gave her a dubious look. He removed a hand from his pocket, slow, and took the card from her. It was grimy, mostly blank. Looked almost homemade. Nothing on it but a number, in deep, black font. And a name. Gil turned it over, expecting more on the back. It was blank.

"I don't get it," he said.

"He helps people," said Mrs. Preston. Her eyebrows yanked themselves up and down, confidential. Her head trembled. As if passing on this knowledge excited but exhausted her. Drained her of some old burden.

Gil looked down again at the card. Its edges frayed. Dark brown spots.

Passed between dozens of hands over dozens of years.

Just a number. And a name.

He tried to hand it back to her. "I don't need a therapist."

She shook her head, put her hands up, palms out. "No, no. You misunderstand. He isn't... He's a kind of healer."

The card lingered in the air between them. Once he realized he was stuck with it, Gil drew it back in. It felt heavier than it had a few seconds ago.

"He helped me understand," she explained, "that when people die, their spirits expand. Swell out of the body into the air. To be part of everything without being bound. That's the beauty of being *released* after death. But if they feel... unfinished, people get stuck. Halfway. They... echo back.

"These echoes aren't contained in bodies anymore, of course, so they become tethered to a specific place. Like your apartment. Sometimes an object, like a mirror. And they sort of... bounce around in there, in that loose, expanded state, instead of swelling into the air and being free. It's *hard*. But this man." She wagged a finger at the card. "He helps set them free. That's where my husband has gone now."

"Gone," said Gil. It was the only word that really stood out.

She nodded. "But gone where he's a *part* of everything, like he's supposed to be. Gone to... to a better place."

"Ah huh." Gil stared at the card. It grew heavier.

"Well, thanks," he said. Immediately he hated himself for sounding disingenuous. "I mean, really. Thank you. I'll... I'll give him a try."

She grinned again. He tried not to look at her teeth, realizing just how grey they were. "Do. He *helps*. He'll help your wife find her way."

"Right. No, I appreciate it. I'll give you the card back after I call him?"

"Oh, no. I don't need it anymore. It's yours."

With that, she waved, wished him good luck, and shut the door. A waft of incense puffed out after her. He coughed.

Gil remained for several seconds, until he heard the chain slide on the other side of the door and figured it was probably time to walk back down the hall. The entire way, he held the card out in front of his chest. Stiff. As if it were on fire.

Nothing there. Except a number. And a name.

When he got home, it took him 10

nervous minutes, one hand holding the card, the other turning in his pocket, to finally take out his phone and dial the number.

It rang twice.

When the line connected, he heard a cough. The crack-rustle of moving leather. Then a voice. Low and thick, like the drone of a distant lawnmower: "Hector Brim. Help you."

Gil swallowed. This was not the voice he'd expected. It did not feel safe. It did not feel helpful. It felt, instead, like someone had stretched rubber bands across his limbs and now tugged them hard.

"Hello," he managed. "My name is, uh, Gil. I have a, a problem."

"Most people do."

This threw him off. "It's... Ah huh. Right. Well. I got this card from a friend. It's my wife. She—"

"When did she pass?"

Again, Gil was taken aback. The voice hadn't skipped a beat. No preamble, no explanations. The blank simplicity of the card made itself felt here, too. This man knew what he was about.

"About a month ago," he said.

"Recent."

A pause. Gil's grip on the phone tightened. He wasn't sure if he was supposed to say something or if the man on the other end were thinking. Or waiting. He pictured the voice out there, what its owner looked like. Saw him sitting in shadow, draped over an armchair in a corner somewhere. Nothing but stillness and dark and—

The voice broke in on him: "Your address?"

Numb, Gil could think of nothing else to do, other than just give it to him.

"Mm. Been there before."

"Yes. Um. Mrs. Preston. She gave me your card."

"Not much for names."

Another pause. Gil winced.

"So," he said.

"Alright. Three hours work for you?"

"Three... Sorry, three hours from now?"

"Mm."

"I." Gil cleared his throat. "Yes. Sorry. Yes. That works."

"Be four hundred."

"Sorry, dollars?"

The line went dead.

Gil began to pace, heart and mind racing. Eventually, he landed on the couch in the living room. Tucked his knees up under his chin. Coiled himself there, tight and anxious. He wondered what he was supposed to do for three hours. Knew he would do nothing but sit.

Regret flooded him.

A better place... Christ, that's... What is that? What a fucking cliché. That might be all well and good for Mr. Preston, but whatever that "better place" was, Natalie would be *gone.* And suddenly, he wasn't so sure he wanted that. Even if it meant hurting her, he wanted her to stay. Because if she left, he'd be totally, completely *alone.*

He thought about asking the light in the hall for its opinion, but was afraid to know the answer.

No. He knew. And he *knew* he knew. This was the right thing to do. He was just scared, that was all.

So he sat. Waiting. His entire body throbbing. Eventually, he got up and wrote a check to Hector Brim.

🕐

When Hector Brim was young, he moved to the city because he wanted to feel connected to everything. All the voices and echoes he could possibly hear. He'd brought with him his bag of Brim family tricks. The tricks were old, but new to him and exciting. For the most part.

There were a few that Hector, for

the several years his father trained him, passing on his inheritance, had never really liked or understood.

The brand, for example.

"Doesn't it hurt?" Hector asked once, when he was nine.

"This tool is for angry, violent spirits," his father explained. "Ones beyond our help, and in need of control."

"But they're people, too."

"Everybody is people, too."

"So, we should help everybody."

His father smiled. A limp, tired thing. "You can try. That's all this family has done, for nearly a century. Try. Come, let's keep practicing. Hold the brand to the light again. Your form needs improvement."

When Hector moved to the city, he rented a small apartment in Chinatown, and everything was magic. This was back when he was helping people, and the irises of his eyes were sunlight on leaves. He looked through them at his new apartment, beaming. They shone as he thought of all those echoes, all the people there to help. All around him, in the tall glittering of the city.

It was a bright time. Being young.

But the more time he spent in that apartment—the more he listened to the radiator's metallic tattoo, the scurry of rats on floorboards, the couple upstairs who fought and broke things, the alley downstairs where people mugged, fucked, wept, vomited—the smaller it felt. More cramped. More lonely.

Jobs poured in. Word of mouth. Desperate people seeking closure, seeking help, seeking proof of Something More.

He kept doing it, dealing out his family tricks like candy. But the high lessened every time. For a while, he brought the stones to the shore every time he used the box for a job. Kept dumping them there, trying to feel good about it all. Trying. He even tried to feel good about the times he had to use the more violent tricks, like the brand.

But something held him back.

One day, before he brought the latest stone to the beach, Hector gazed out his one small window at the afternoon. He held the stone in his hand, soaking in its warmth and company, its voice.

He always liked to sit with them like that. Just for a little while. The company was good, for what it was. The sun gleamed against all the glass stuck up in the sky. He tried to breathe it in. Feel less cramped. Tried to press his palm against the window and touch it all. All those people....

But the family tricks don't work that way.

His eyes landed on a face. Stuck inside another window, far across the way, gaping out at the same bleak cityscape. And seeing that, Hector realized that he wasn't connected to anything at all. He was in a cage. His palm against the bars. That face was in its own cage. And all across the city, there was nothing at all but cage upon cage upon cage. All alone. All clanking, scurrying, fighting, breaking, mugging, fucking, crying, dying. No trick could help or stop that. He realized this, and something inside of him began to turn. To bend.

He never took that stone to the beach.

Eventually, his entire world became nothing more than the warm-metal piss-stink of a life lived in a constrictive, concrete Hell.

And that was a very long time ago.

☉

Gil opened the door. He had to take a step back and blink. Looking at Hector Brim gave him vertigo. The doorway swam a little, and it took him a moment to steady it. The man was well past six feet tall, looming a solid foot over Gil. He was old. Tufts of dirty-snow hair cotton-balled across his head. The vertigo came not from his height but from his body, which was cracked to one side.

Head lilting towards his left shoulder, and the shoulder sagging outward. It was the bag in the man's left hand. It dragged an entire half of his body down towards the floor. A massive, black leather briefcase. Stuffed with what Gil assumed could only be bricks. The man's eyes made Gil dizzy, too. The irises a deep, vague moss. Overgrown and forgotten. The man's beige trench coat must have weighed a ton. And it was August.

The man spoke. "Gil?" That old lawn-mower groan.

"I am. Yes." Gil stuck out his hand. Hector Brim stared at it. Gil retracted.

"Come in," he said. "Mister...."

"Just Brim."

Brim had to duck under the doorway. He stepped into the room, feet heavy, echoing. Gil closed the door behind him. As soon as Brim entered the apartment, he locked his eyes on the ceiling. Grunted. Moved into the living room. The carcass of the piano was still in the corner, but Brim didn't even glance at it. He moved in slow circles around the room, gazing up at the ceiling. The bag thudded against his thigh, but he seemed not to mind. He'd done this hundreds of times before. Thousands, maybe.

The room was silent except for the soft pound of the bag and the flutter of the trench coat. Gil stood awkwardly by the door, hands shoved into the pockets of his jeans. Should he say something? Brim didn't seem to mind the quiet, so Gil remained silent. Brim swung his head from side to side. It swung him into the hall, and his body followed it, as if the rest of his spine were only vaguely attached to his skull. A broken rag doll, Gil thought. He hesitated, then followed in Brim's wake. When he did, he found Brim standing in the middle of the hall, staring straight up. Straight into the light fixture.

"Jesus," Gil couldn't stop himself from muttering. "That's her."

"Seems like."

"I mean... You're the real deal. Aren't you?"

"Never heard anything to the contrary." Brim kept his eyes on the light.

Gil became immediately aware that Nat was hiding. That she was pointedly not making herself known. She didn't want to go. She wasn't ready to leave him. He could feel it. His hands turned in his pockets. Anxiety tugged at those rubber bands in his arms. He shuddered.

"Woman down the hall," said Brim.

"Um. Mrs. Preston."

Brim grimaced. "Names...."

Gil wasn't sure what he meant by that.

"She explain to you?" Brim asked. "About souls?"

"She said something about expansion? I mean, no, not really. I... Look—"

"Mm." Brim lurched back into the living room. He breezed past Gil, pressing him against the wall. The bag almost rammed into Gil's knee as he passed. Again, Gil followed. He felt stupid just following this man around his apartment, but he wasn't sure what else he was supposed to be doing.

"Souls," said Brim. He positioned himself in the middle of the living room, and Gil felt his blood go cold. Brim stood in the exact center of where the heart had been. Maybe Brim already knew that. That was probably the point.

In his pockets, Gil's hands churned.

"When our bodies release them," Brim continued, "they spiral out into the ether." He placed his briefcase on the floor. "Typically, they go elsewhere. Don't know much about *that*."

He undid the zipper running along the top of the briefcase. Its lips yawned open. Gil could almost hear it sigh. "But if there is a lack of what you might call *closure*, the spirit remains. In a somewhat half-tethered, expanded state. Your wife, for instance."

The bag looked like it was choking. It gasped for air. Jaw muscles stretched tight against whatever was lodged in its throat. Gil felt it, like a living thing. He stepped back. "Your wife has *expanded* out of her body, and has sunken herself into the very beams of your home. It is, I'm sure, uncomfortable." Brim reached down into the gaping maw of the bag. It seemed to gag around his wrist. Gil took another step back. "What we do here is re-condense those souls. Bind them back into something more... solid." Brim pulled a box out of the bag's innards. He held it up and looked at it.

The box was an ancient thing. It had the same passed-down quality of Brim's card. Its sides shone black from decades of hands. The small brass latch had once glittered, but now bore the dull refraction of a dying fluorescent.

Brim placed the box on the floor next to the bag. He slid open the latch, lifted the lid. Let it fall back. The box and the bag sat next to each other, yawning at the ceiling. Trying to swallow it whole.

"The box will accomplish that," Brim concluded. He ambled over to the couch. Sat down with a large rush of air. He sighed. The coat settled about him. He was still.

Gil stared at him. Almost a minute passed. Brim sat motionless, hands in his lap. Eyes blank. Gil shifted side to side. Part of him wanted to grab the ax again and hack the little box apart. Silence throbbed against his ears until, finally, he burst.

"I don't understand what the fuck is happening."

Brim jerked his shoulders. "Your wife will condense inside the box. I'll take her to a place where she can be free. She'll be ready in a minute or two."

"Yeah, sorry, I don't know what the fuck that means, though." Anger curled into Gil's voice. Brim just stared at him, unmoved. Those old moss-covered rocks gaping out from their sockets.

Gil stepped forward. Took his hands out of his pockets. "Hey. What does that *mean*?"

Brim sighed again. Everything seemed hard to him. Everything a struggle. He seemed to drag himself through talking just like he dragged his body through space.

"Look, don't bother asking how it works, because I don't know. Just that it does. The box draws souls inside itself. Once inside the box, they crystalize into stones. The stone usually reflects the true spirit of the person. Agate, pyrite, opal, amazonite, obsidian, red coral.... Most people are quartzite." He shook his head. "You wouldn't *believe* how many people are quartzite."

"I don't give a shit about quartzite. I know my wife. I don't need to see her true whatever the fuck."

"Not about need. Happen anyway." The final word strained as Brim stood. He unbent himself from the couch and his joints cracked. He shuffled back to the box, continuing to crack and pop along the way. He towered above the ancient, wooden thing. Peered into it.

"Ah," he said. He stooped, reached inside.

Gil felt manic. Felt angry energy beating through his body like massive drums. He was restless and tired and he wanted this man gone. He wanted his wife back. Wanted her to stay. Not *crystallized*. Fuck this. He charged to the door, threw it open, and said, voice shaking, "You know what? This, this is done. I'm sorry. I don't want this."

Brim didn't move. He kept his hand in the box.

"Hey. Did you hear me? I—"

"Tiger's eye."

Gil blinked. "I'm sorry?"

"Tiger's eye." Brim held up a gleaming, honey-colored stone, about the size of his thumb.

Gil swallowed. "Where... where did that come from? How did you get that? What is that?" His mind rejected it. This rock was not his wife.

Brim ignored him. "Tiger's eye is a good one. Your wife was very confident."

Gil shook his head. "Stop."

"She was grounded. Practical. Had an artistic streak."

"Please stop."

"She made you feel safe. Brought good luck."

"I said *stop*."

"Here."

Brim strode over to Gil. He held out the stone. Eels swarmed in Gil's stomach. He hesitated. He gave Brim his hand. Brim placed the stone in Gil's palm. It was warm. Felt... full.

"Can you feel her?" Brim asked.

Gil's voice came from far away. "Yes."

"Can you hear her?"

His eyes burned. He didn't move his hand. He felt the warmth, the pulse of those ribbons of color. Tried to focus, and feel or hear anything else.

"No," he said. His voice caught in his throat.

"I can. She has a beautiful voice. Hearing her sing must have been very special."

Gil looked up. The man's face remained mossy and distant.

"What are you going to do with her?" Gil asked. "I mean, how does this help her? She's *in* there? Fucking... *in* there?"

"I'll take her to the beach. Many other stones. There, she can be with the ocean and the land and everything else. Free. Connected to the entire world."

"Oh," said Gil. He didn't take his eyes off the stone.

After a long time, Brim slid it from Gil's hand. "It's time."

Gil felt suddenly cold and empty.

"I can take her to the beach," he said, desperate. "Let me take her."

Brim shook his head. "There's another step."

"Can I at least wa—"

"It must be done alone. It's how the trick works."

Gil shrank. "Oh."

"Don't worry. She'll be fine. Think of it like spreading your ashes into the ocean."

"I... I like that."

"Most people do."

These were the last words they exchanged. Brim slipped the stone into the breast pocket of his coat. With it, Gil felt like his soul slipped away, too. He opened his mouth. Nothing came. He closed it.

Brim gathered up his bag, gagging it again with the box and sealing its lips with the old, bulging zipper. Gil watched, feeling empty. Not sure what else to do. He gave Brim the check. And the man was gone, thumping out the door with his bag. Quiet and somehow shameful, like he'd just broken Gil's heart. And Gil, just as ashamed, slumped back onto the couch. Coiled himself back up. The walls closed on him.

The apartment was empty. Down to its very beams. For the first time since the funeral, he felt truly, irrevocably alone. An animal in a cage. He told himself that it was the right thing. That she would be alright. That he. would be alright. He told himself everything was fine. Everything was good.

And then he wept.

Outside, lurching through the hall, Brim heard him. He smiled. He knew that feeling. And it was so delicious to feel it spread around him like a weed.

🕓

Hector Brim never went to the beach. Instead, he dragged himself along the subway, back to his hot, cramped apartment. Bag kept him lopsided, whacking against his leg as the subway moved. Sometimes he thought about not bringing it. Bringing just the box. He usually just needed the box. But you never knew. If the woman had been stubborn, he'd have needed the lighter, the saw. Maybe even the brand. Best to be prepared.

Scraping down the street, bag thumping at him. August, and the trenchcoat, made Brim sweat. Could take it off for once. But without the coat, he wouldn't have his father's echo, which was company at least.

The echo kept asking *why*.

Rolled his shoulder back. Rolled the voice out of his mind. Didn't need the judgement. Just the company.

Back at his building. Not as nice a place as Gil's. No tall ceilings. No elevator. Everything here warped, curling wood. The floor didn't reflect or clap as you walked on it. It screamed.

Key stuck in the lock. Door stuck on the jamb. AC leaking on the floor, broken.

The coat twitched. It called him back to the beach. Tried to remind him this wasn't what the family tricks were for.

Tried.

Hector took off the coat and the echo vanished. He hung it on a hook by the door. Limped into his main room. Turned and stood before the large glass table. Perfect, unstained. Ancient. Passed down, like almost everything else here. And resting in its center, the massive glass bowl.

That was Hector's, and Hector's alone.

Hector dropped his bag on the floor. He stepped out of his loafers, nudged them against the wall. Gray-blue balls of hairy dust fluttered in his wake. He moved back down the hall, to the coat. Reached inside the pocket. As he brushed against the fabric, he heard the faint echo-cry of his father. Ignored it. Removed the chunk of tiger's eye from the pocket. Moved away. Returned to the table. The bowl.

He ran the warm stone between his fingers. Felt the woman in there. Heard her. He held her above the bowl for a moment. Listening. Watching. Feeling her through his fingers. She was attractive, and he could feel her throwing herself around with that confidence and will tiger's eye usually indicated. She *did* have a beautiful voice. Probably wonderful to hear her sing. But it was even more beautiful to hear her scream. Beautiful to hear her trapped inside that tiny stone room. Afraid. Confused. Beating her head against its sides, unable to understand the cage she'd been sucked into. Utterly alone. In the dark. Lost and hurting and scared and, above all, stuck there for eternity.

He smiled.

He dropped her into the bowl.

She clattered down against hundreds of others. Brilliant colors flashed through the glass. Purple, blue, green, red, and orange. Bright white and pitch black. Stones of every kind. Quartzite. There was a *lot* of quartzite.

Hector's fingers itched with excitement. He grinned, wide and wolfish. He let himself linger there, fingers twitching over the rim of the bowl, for as long as he could stand. This was the best part of the day. He savored it. Then plunged his hand inside. The roar was orgasmic. Thousands of voices, all howling, weeping. All of them stuck in the dark. Stuck inside their little stones.

He closed his eyes. Lost himself in the wash of voices. In the wash of power over each and every soul. His knees began to quake. A cacophony of wails. All those people condensed into tiny dark hells. Sucked into the box against their will and beaten into rock. Trapped in some cramped, intangible vessel, with nothing but four walls and a hard floor. Unable to see or feel or understand beyond its bonds. They did not sleep. Did not hunger. Nothing to break the monotony except tears and the memory of light.

Hector had to sit down. He kept one hand in the bowl, fingers hot against the spirits of the many-dead. Reached around blind for a chair with the other hand. Dragged it to him. Dropped into it. Sighed. The euphoria. The *company* of this bowl. All locked in their own little cages. All hopeless and trapped, echoing *him*. His own ache. That was good. *So* good. Good to not feel *alone*.

He licked his lips. Swam his fingers around. The stones clicked and beat against each other. Screams faded and grew as he grazed against each soul.

This, he thought. *This* was the true connection. The heart of everything human. Suffering and shadow.

Somewhere in the back of his mind, his father's voice still begged. Told him, for the millionth time, that this was not why the tricks had been passed down. They were passed down to *help* people.

When you were young, Hector, you understood. So why this? What happened?

Who the hell knows, he said, and shoved his father out of his skull.

His hand stopped. His thumb had landed against one piece in particular. Hector fished it out of the bowl. Held it above the rim. Looked at it. It was cold. Lifeless. He had to squeeze it hard to feel the soul inside. What a coincidence. Mr. Preston. Huddled deep into the rock. Closed in on himself in the corner of his cage. Silent and limp.

Hector remembered him now. Remembered how the man used to thrash. To beg. All quiet now.

Sometimes this happened. Sometimes so much time had passed, and so much despair spent, that the souls inside the stones faded. Stopped crying or trying to escape or anything else. They just stopped. Sat down. Grew cold. Remained there. Staring at the walls. Forever.

Hector understood. It happens.

He popped the stone into his mouth. Crunched Mr. Preston between his teeth, ground him into nothing, and swallowed him out of existence.

Whatever beauty there was in the world, Hector Brim never felt like he had been made privy to it. But at least he could try to make himself feel better.

Try.

He closed his eyes, and dove his hand back into the bowl.

Except the sound of stones running between his fingers, the little apartment was silent. Upstairs, the couple still fought, after all this time. Down in the alley, a pregnant homeless girl vomited.

Everyone everywhere alone.

≩ASHLEY NAFTULE≩

A THOUSAND CRANES OF BLOOD AND STEEL

ILLUSTRATIONS BY CAMILLE VILLANUEVA

"Pens and swords. Nobody ever talks about paper."

Okada ran the bolt of burgundy cloth through his fingers, nodding with approval. He didn't need to see the machine that printed it to know it was high-quality work. After 35 years working as a combat tailor, his fingertips could tease out the potential of anything that crossed his worktable.

"I'm not following," Thorne said. Okada had a habit of blurting out non sequiturs while they worked. The hardest lesson Quinlan Thorne learned during his apprenticeship with The Iron Dressmaker was to not even try and guess what his master was talking about. In three years, he'd never guessed right.

"That old bullshit about the pen and the sword," Okada said, folding the cloth in half. He ran a worn bone folder down the length of the cloth, creating a crease sharp enough to cut through glass. Most tailors switched out their folders every five years or so; Okada still used the same one his mother passed down to him when he graduated from finishing school.

"Right, the one where the pen is mightier," Thorne murmured, patting down the length of his tool-corset for a pair of tweezers.

Okada grunted. "If the pen's mightier than the sword, where does that leave paper?"

Thorne hated riddles; trying to solve them felt like folding his brain into shapes it was never meant to take on. "In the same state as flesh?"

The Iron Dressmaker reached out and pulled a ribbon of Vantablack silk across the table, layering it on top of the burgundy fold. "The fuck are you on about?" A quick drag of the bone folder and the Vantablack was seared into the middle of the burgundy, creating a perfect black void in its midsection.

"Well, I mean... flesh and paper are at the mercy of sword and pen, right? Canvases to be written on?" Thorne knew it wasn't the right thing to say, but it felt as good an answer as any.

Okada shook his head. "They're the same thing. Paper and the sword. In my culture, we treat them the same."

Before Thorne could say anything, Okada's hands moved like a blur across the cloth. His hands twisted and folded it into a sleeve.

"To make a sword out of jewel steel,

you have to fold the metal. Many times. The steel gets folded over and over again until its true strength, its true form, emerges."

Okada rose from the table and walked over to the sword hanging on the wall. "Quinlan, the sleeve."

Thorne set his work aside and reached for the testing smock. Slipping the smock over his body and fixing the mask to his face, he went to pick up the burgundy and Vantablack sleeve. It felt as light and insubstantial as cobwebs.

"The same with paper," Okada said. "To make origami, we fold the kami until it becomes what it's supposed to be. A single compressed line, like the steel. Folded and folded until it becomes something sharp and beautiful."

Okada unsheathed the sword with a flick of his wrist. In one smooth motion he swung the blade down onto the fabric and the katana shattered. Gleaming fragments of steel rained down onto the floor. Thorne could see himself reflected in the shards, still holding the intact sleeve.

The master ran his thumb across the cloth, shaking his head with disapproval. Thorne knew that look well—when he first started learning from the master, Okada had him fold a thousand paper cranes. The Iron Dressmaker inspected every single one of them; the only ones he'd accept were the ones sharp enough to draw blood. Thorne never forgot the cruel smile that flickered across Okada's face after he finished his 800th bloody crane and asked his master why it had to be a thousand.

"There's a legend in my culture that says anyone who folds a thousand paper cranes will be granted a wish by the gods," Okada said, admiring the blood staining a crane's beak. "If you really want to learn from me, boy, you better wish for it."

The sour grimace on Okada's face migrated to his brow as he let go of the sleeve, his forehead creasing into a deep frown. "The fold on this one is flawed. The sword should have snapped at least two seconds earlier. I must be losing my touch."

Another important lesson Thorne learned in his apprenticeship: No one could live up to the standards of the master. Not even the master himself.

"Fuck it. The next one will be better." The Iron Dressmaker tossed the sleeve into the recycler. "Quinlan, before I forget: we're out of swords. Have them print us another two dozen."

"Whiskey sour, dirty. I like to see my drinks."

It was Thorne's first night off in a month. Okada's shop had been working on the winter line for six months straight to finish outfits for the Martial Ball. The Pacific Coalition's Defense Secretary had offered Okada a five-year exclusive contract after last year's Ball, and the master was working everyone ragged to make sure this year's ballistic fashion was up to snuff. He wasn't about to give Secretary Kalatozovl buyer's remorse.

The bartender slipped a smoke cartridge into Thorne's hookah. Vaporized whiskey sour, blended together with a potent strain of Europa kush. Most people ordered their inhales clean, but Thorne liked being able to breath out smoke like a dragon. He even liked the ragged coughing fits that shook his body after a few deep hits.

"I like your sarong. Is that panther?"

It was the woman three chairs down. Thorne saw her when he walked in, a short redhead in a cowboy shirt and blue jeans. She had cat's eyes and an animated tattoo of a yellow circle that drifted around her neck. Sneaking glances at her throughout the night, Thorne saw the circle eat little white dots as it chased after a multicolored group of ghosts. Sometimes the ghosts would eat the circle and it would turn into a dot, too.

"You've got a good eye," Thorne said. "I skinned it two years ago. Sewed and folded it myself."

The woman narrowed her eyes, letting a small plume of smoke pass through her lips. Thorne breathed it in: gin and tonic.

"Was the cat vat-grown, or original flavor?"

Thorne laughed so hard it rattled his earrings. "I don't know anyone with a credit rating good enough to see a natural panther, let alone kill one."

They both smiled, breathing in each other's smoke.

"Monica," she said. The yellow circle had come back to life, gobbling up a cherry that was drifting around her neck. She held her hand out and nodded twice, signaling her consent.

"Quinlan," he said, bending low to plant a kiss on her knuckles.

Monica pointed to the sewing needle pierced above Thorne's collarbone. "You're a tailor."

He scanned her body, searching for signs of guild affiliation. Nothing. "You're a freelancer."

Monica nodded. "I'm a journalist by day." She gestured to the bartender. "Gimme an old man drink. I want to smell like my grandfather."

"And what are you by night?" Thorne asked. He looked at her jeans and noticed a stiffness to the cut. He wondered if they were bulletproof.

"Just a regular old busybody," she said. "You any good at what you do?"

Thorne shrugged. "Show me a landmine and I can show you a pair of heels I've made that can tango on top of it without losing a toe."

The bartender switched out their cartridges. Monica took a long pull from her hookah and coughed out whiskey sour as Thorne breathed in a gin and tonic. She lifted her left leg and let her pump hit the floor. Thorne could see three chrome toes wiggling in the bar sign's neon light.

"I wish they carried your shoes in Cambodia."

⊕

Thorne had been to seven Martial Balls before as a spectator, apprentice, and now a journeyman. The pageantry of diplomacy, arms-testing, and ballroom dancing should have been old hat by now. But this was the first time he had brought along a date, so everything felt new.

Monica and Thorne wore matching top hats and tuxedo gowns. The hats were Monica's idea—an homage to Marlene Dietrich, whoever that was. Getting her security clearance to attend the Ball took some doing, but luckily she knew a freelancer who served with Secretary Kalatazov during the Battle of Naypyidaw.

"Syd was one of the last people out of Myanmar before they dropped the bubble over it," Monica had told him on the drive over. "It was her job to watch the feeds coming out of the containment field. She said it took less than 48 hours before they resorted to cannibalism."

Thorne had visited the Myanmar bubble once, a few months after the Pacific Coalition started letting civilians get within a few miles of it. He still thought about all the bloody handprints he saw imprinted on the crackling energy field—the desperation of trapped, starving people tattooed onto the air.

He had tried to spot signs of life through the bubble, but Naypyidaw stayed silent and still before him. For a moment, Thorne had felt a flash of resentment course through him, the same bitter disappointment that would seize him as a child when he went to the zoo and didn't see any animals because they were sleeping out of sight in the shade. Remembering his sense of entitlement, his outrage at being denied a moment of grisly sightseeing, filled him with shame.

Thank God I'm not dating a telepath, Thorne thought as Monica placed her hand on the small of his back.

The Martial Ball was a different kind of bubble—less bloody but just as impenetrable to outsiders. A vast ballroom teeming with security drones, reporters, officers, models, and starlets, it was full of the only air worth breathing: the kind that fills the lungs of the rarefied and classified.

Thorne and Monica weaved their way through the crowd, brushing past

five-star generals flirting with synthetic courtesans. Thorne could see Okada across the room; his master was having an animated talk with the Secretary. Okada had gone Retro-Macho with his aesthetic: Led Zeppelin T-shirt, leather pants, sneakers, and a cowboy hat. He looked gauche and ridiculous, as he always did at these events.

"If you look like a peasant, they won't expect you to make work worthy of royalty," Okada had confided to him once, after a drunken night of saki smoke and fried octopus. "I like to get their expectations so low I can step on them."

Secretary Kalatazov wore his dress pinks, ironed and pressed to perfection. Judging from the way he was looking at Okada's hat, Thorne guessed the Secretary's expectations were low enough to limbo under a cockroach's belly.

"That's him, isn't it? The Iron Dressmaker?"

Monica pointed out Okada with her long cigarette holder. The tip of it housed a burnt nub of hashish that glowed faintly. Wisps of smoke curled from the end of it. They looked like beckoning fingers to Thorne. Come hither.

"The one and only."

She squinted at Okada, who was doubled over laughing, holding onto the Secretary's arm to steady himself.

"He's not what I expected."

Thorne grabbed a pair of drinks off a waiter's tray. "I'll tell him you said that. He'll take it as a compliment."

Monica downed her fizzy drink in one gulp. "Didn't he wear assless chaps to one of these things?"

Thorne almost choked on his drink. "Thanks for reminding me. I had burnt the memory out of my brain."

Monica took a deep drag, exhaling another crooked finger into the rarefied and classified air.

"That must be nice, being able to burn your memories out. All of mine are branded in."

⊕

The fashion show was always the best part of the Martial Ball. This year's was no different.

Thorne sat to Okada's left while Secretary Kalatazov took his right, fanning himself with a lace fan. Kalatazov's wife, boyfriend, and mistress sat behind them. Monica, three drinks into the festivities, rested her head on Thorne's shoulder. Her top hat hung off the side of her head like it was glued on.

Male, female, and non-binary soldiers marched briskly across the runway. Most of the tailored armor dresses, sarongs, and catsuits were red and white—the colors of the Pacific Coalition. But a few of the more eye-catching designs were decked out in burgundy and Vantablack shades. They were the Secretary's favorite colors.

"These designs are gorgeous," Kalatazov whispered to Okada. His face beamed with amazement at the enlisted models parading in front of him. Thorne saw the faintest trace of a smirk creep across Okada's face. No doubt the Iron Dressmaker was enjoying the sound of Kalatazov's expectations crunching beneath his feet.

"And they are battle ready?"

Okada grinned at the Secretary's question. "All of my babies are fashionable and tactical. The ones that aren't get smothered in the crib."

Thorne felt a tug on his arm. "Where's the latrine, corporal tailor?"

He reached back and gestured to the pearl-handled doors at the back of the room. Monica planted a quick kiss on his cheek and snuck away. Thorne watched her disappear into the standing room crowd. He felt like the hashish smoke was still in the air, beckoning him to follow her.

Okada elbowed him gently in the ribs. "Here comes your masterpiece." It was a tease, but there was real affection in his master's voice.

A seven-foot model strutted down the runway, wearing a ballistic corset and a minesweeper hoop skirt. It had taken Thorne three months to get the design right. Seeing it in motion on a living breathing human being, he saw that it was time well-spent.

The Secretary whooped with delight. "This one! I want one for my wife, one for my man, and one for all my guards."

Kalatazov clapped Okada on the back. Delighted, the Iron Dressmaker returned the gesture. And that's when the Defense Secretary's head exploded.

⊕

It took forensics three hours to thoroughly examine the ballroom. Which meant that Thorne had to sit there, immobilized in his chair, for three hours while covered in pieces of Kalatazov's skull. Security drones and military police locked down the room moments after the Secretary's head detonated. Everyone inside was frozen in place, paralyzed by the nanites housed inside their attendee wristbands.

Thorne considered himself lucky that he had Okada as a buffer. His master was coated with gore, his face stuck in a rictus of shock and disgust. One of Kalatazov's eyeballs had landed on the brim of Okada's cowboy hat. The pupil pointed down; it almost looked like it was trying to meet Okada's horrified stare.

Frozen in place, the stench of burnt flesh and viscera in his nostrils, Thorne thought about the thing on Monica's neck. The hungry little circle chasing ghosts. He wondered if the circle ever got to eat the ghosts, or if he was doomed to forever be devoured by them.

When the nanites were deactivated, they were taken in one by one for questioning. As the people closest to the Secretary, Okada and Thorne were the first ones taken in. Thorne didn't remember the interrogation. He had gone through the process in the past, and it was always the same: the signing of the waiver, the injection of the truth serum, and then the blackout. He woke up outside the interrogation chambers, a chip containing the video file of the interrogation tagged and bagged in his hand.

He waited for Okada to be released, turning the chip over in his hands. He didn't worry about what was on there— if they were going to pin this on him, he would have already been moved off-site.

Thorne didn't bother trying to make sense of how Kalatazov died. He had heard enough war stories from clients and fellow tailors who had served in Australia and Cambodia to figure out what killed the Secretary. It was something

small and folded in on itself, over and over again until it achieved its perfect state, just like kami and jewel steel.

Sitting in that off-white room, hair still matted with clumps of blood, Thorne thought about his masterpiece. The corset, the hoop skirt, the luminous obsidian skin of the lieutenant model. Anything to burn the memory of Kalatazov's eyeball perched atop a cowboy hat out of his brain.

🕐

Okada and Thorne shared a ride back to their hotel in silence. He had known the Iron Dressmaker for long enough to know what was written on his face. Okada was worried about what the glossy magazines would say. Assassinations always brought bad reviews, no matter how good the show was. And Thorne didn't need to know Morse code to interpret the message Okada kept tapping on his leather-clad knee. There goes our contract. Six months of work for a bloody curtain call.

He was relieved that Okada didn't ask him about Monica. That wasn't a conversation Thorne wanted to have with anyone just yet. At his apartment, Thorne took the elevator up to his floor. It took three waves before the unit's chip reader synced with the one planted in the palm of his hand and opened the door.

Her stuff was still there. A part of him thought about going through her bags, searching for some kind of clue. A reason why she was the only one unaccounted for after the explosion. An explanation for why her security wristband was lying on the bathroom floor. Maybe even a note revealing how she was able to sneak the spore-sized, remote detonated bomb into Kalatazov's drink.

He left everything as it was. Security would come soon enough. They would unfold the mystery. Thorne went to the bathroom and turned on the shower. He left his bloody clothes on the floor.

He dug his fingers in tight as he scrubbed the blood out of his hair. He imagined folding himself. Twisting his head into cubist shapes, forming geometrically perfect creases across the crown of his skull, folding himself into his perfect form. For one moment, his skin was as supple and rich and pliable as the beautiful fabrics in Okada's workshop. But no matter how much he folded himself, he couldn't get it quite right—even in his imagination he was always one or two steps away from perfection.

=JOSHUAH STOLAROFF=

GHOSTS OF LONE PINE

ILLUSTRATIONS BY CAMILLE VILLANUEVA

Randy Leeworth's knee hurt. But he hadn't missed his walk to the top of Owl Ridge in fifteen years, and he didn't intend to turn around now, halfway up. He paused and removed his cowboy hat, smoothing his long, gray hair while he surveyed the direction from which he'd come. Behind him was a slope of gravel and sagebrush, contoured by the early morning sun, then his little ranch house, with its corral and garden. He turned and looked up to the ridge.

"Hang in there," he said, thumping his knee. "You ain't *that* old."

Randy continued along the sandy trail, a trail carved by his own steps. The knee only hurt when he put pressure on it, especially when he climbed uphill. He tried to shrug it off. Eyes up. Nothing to whine about. Not like Lester's hip keeping him house-bound. *That* was a trouble.

Randy stepped faster and climbed, his lungs beginning to pull hard on the cool spring air. He knew it was a little worse than yesterday, and had been getting worse for weeks. In a darker moment, he had looked up the next date that agents from the Rural

Outreach Administration were coming through town, and made an appointment. It was scheduled for later this morning, his first in three years.

Randy reached the ridge, leaned against a rock, and shook out his leg. He looked up at the eastern side of the Sierra Nevada mountains, with their shining, granite peaks and tree-dotted foothills. Below that spread the desert floor of Owens Valley with a few ranches, the neglected town of Lone Pine, and the old highway that ran through it. It was the view that reminded him why he lived here.

Randy inspected the highway. As usual, it was empty at first, and then the ghost drivers came into view. They glinted like gravel in the sun, bright and clear at certain angles, blending in with the ruined asphalt at others. They went mostly in fossil-burning vehicles from the last century, but also capsule bikes and hydrogen trucks. They moved smooth and straight, without heed of potholes, fissures, or sand washes. They drove on the highway as it must have been in their time, a speedy thoroughfare to somewhere else.

Randy shook his head. He still didn't know where the ghosts were going. They passed in both directions, mostly single drivers, sometimes families, sometimes cargo trucks.

He looked back to mountain peaks, took a deep breath, and drank in the view. Then Randy turned and walked back home. After breakfast, he saddled up Blackeye, put a pair of empty saddlebags on her, and headed out for his errands.

On the way to town, Randy stopped to see his friend Lester Ghosh. He hitched Blackeye, his sweet-tempered palomino, in the shade of a cottonwood tree. Randy gave her mane a few affectionate strokes and went to Lester's front porch. Avoiding the two fallen steps, he knocked on the door and waited patiently while Lester tapped his way over, cane traversing threadbare rugs and dusty wood floor.

"Randy, my good man, my loyal ally. Please." Lester motioned Randy inside. "Enter my castle and avail yourself of its many luxuries."

"Hi Lester." Randy stepped inside.

"Would you care for an exotic delicacy from a faraway land? I have just prepared a stimulating brew of the arabica bean."

"I see you're on the classics again. No, thanks. I've got an appointment in town."

"An appointment? What important business have you, pray-tell?"

"Going to go see the doc about my knee."

"ROA, eh?" He pronounced the acronym for the Rural Outreach Administration 'row-uh,' as was customary. "I try to have as little business as possible with the carpetbaggers."

"So I've heard."

"But do tell them, if the topic arises, that I am in excellent health, and that my new rose garden has outdone all my previous efforts."

"If it comes up."

"Oh, and you may mention that I single-handedly repaired cracks in the foundation and leaks in the roof."

"Maybe we shouldn't overdo it."

"Quite right, good sir. Stick to the rose garden."

Randy smiled, then paused. "How is the revolution coming?"

Lester was now at the counter that separated the kitchen and living room, and he poured coffee for himself. He was short and round, wearing brown trousers and a gray, robe-like sweater. Wisps of white hair remained on his otherwise brown, bald head. Leaning his cane against a stool, he took a sip and gestured grandly with his free hand.

"It is slow work, but every day is progress." Lester spent a lot of time on the Bluenet with groups of anarcho-socialists and armchair political theorists. Mostly old grouches like him who had read too many books. "Once people understand that authoritarian control is no longer needed for fair allocation of resources, they naturally come around to our side. It's just a matter of getting them to question the status quo."

"Naturally. Have you got the empties?"

"Indeed, my good sir. Just here." Lester motioned to the other side of the counter and began moving toward it.

"I'll get it," Randy said, crossing the aging but tidy living room to save Lester from fetching it. He knew that every step pained Lester, though Lester hid it well.

Randy picked up the canvas bag, which held several jars and tins. It was about a year ago that Lester decided he could no longer walk the one kilometer to the general store. Randy had been bringing him groceries twice a week since then.

"And the refuse, if you please."

He pointed to a smaller burlap bag. Randy picked up the collection meant for the reclaimer.

"Anything else you need?" Randy asked. "I'll be back in the afternoon."

"As king of this fine castle, I want for little."

"That's good." Randy went back to the door and replaced his hat.

"But if you might... reprint those books." Lester pointed to a stack of three leather-bound volumes by the door. Randy reached down for them. "The new titles are written on the note."

Randy's appetite for paper-style books alone probably paid the lease on the general store's reprinter.

"Sure thing, old friend," Randy said. "Farewell."

Randy mounted up and headed for town, avoiding the crumbling road and following a familiar trail along a small arroyo canyon. Lester was the reason Randy found himself in Owens Valley at all. They had met decades ago, when Randy was working kitchens in San Francisco, but then had gone their wandering ways. After chasing girls and working restaurants all up the West Coast, then riding restless and working farms all over the Northwest plains, Randy had been thinking about taking a lease out somewhere and finally settling down. That's when Lester called again. He told Randy about the place he'd found here. Lester said the land had the same clear, quiet presence that he'd always seen behind Randy's eyes.

So Randy had no problem bringing Lester his groceries and helping out with the house. But he worried what would happen when Lester's condition got worse. Lester was afraid to get treatment, because if the government knew he couldn't take care of himself and the property, he'd lose his lease. They'd ship him to Los Angeles or Reno, give him a box in one of those mouse-smelling apartment buildings with a view of weeds and broken concrete. Would it be so bad for him? Maybe not. He would still have his books and his Bluenet. He'd get health care, basic income, public transport.

That was the bargain. The government just couldn't afford to maintain a country built for ten times as many people. So they set up Service Areas, mostly in cities, and said, "Hey, you want roads, water, education, free housing? Live in a Service Area. You want to live outside the Service Area? Okay. We'll lease you land and a building for free, but you've got to maintain it, and you get nothing else. Except a once-a-month visit from ROA."

Randy had tried both sides, and he settled on option two. He couldn't blame Lester for wanting to stay out of the cities. Beside that, Lester's parents were both refugees from the Bengali floods, back in the early Contraction. People forget the terrible things that happened to migrants in those days, back before countries started falling over themselves to welcome every live person they could get. But Lester's parents lived it, and Lester grew up hearing those stories. A basic distrust of authority was something that he and Randy shared—Lester, because of his parents, and Randy, because he grew up Out-Service. So of course Randy would help Lester stay put.

🕐

Blackeye ambled around a bend in the canyon, and then Randy saw them: a whole group of ghosts, only fifteen meters away. They were native ghosts, Panamint tribe, if Randy had read his history right. Three of them were standing and three were crouching near the edge of the dry creek. Two more were bent over the creek bed, as if splashing their faces. In their era, this creek would have been flowing with snowmelt. It would have been a nice place to stop on their spring migration across the valley.

Randy took tighter hold of the reins. He wasn't worried about the ghosts for his sake; they never noticed him, but occasionally they took an interest in Blackeye, and she could get spooked. He hurried Blackeye along the trail, which took them closer to the ghosts but stayed on the opposite side of the creek. Then one of the standing ghosts, a teenage boy, turned and looked Randy right in the eyes.

The boy turned his head to watch Randy pass. He looked curious.

Randy startled and kicked Blackeye into a trot until they were well past. That was strange. Randy had seen native ghosts, cowboy ghosts, and plenty of modern ones around here. Usually not as close. Still, he never thought the ghosts could see him. Maybe the boy just saw Blackeye and looked to where the rider would be? "I guess I was the one who got spooked," he said to Blackeye.

It hadn't always been like this. Randy had only begun seeing ghosts a few years ago. Ghosts, or echoes, or whatever they were. He hadn't always been burdened with visions of the past. Had he? Something about the way the boy looked at him reminded Randy about the feeling he used to get sometimes, an unsettled sadness when turning a corner on the street or walking into a room. Maybe that's why he drank so much when he lived in cities. Maybe that's why he took the toughest jobs and worked all the shifts.

Soon, Randy came to the center of town, though town was a generous term for Lone Pine, with its two running businesses and an ROA office open once a month. But then, people called a lot of places towns that really weren't anymore. At least it wasn't a ghost town. Or, not only.

Blackeye click-clacked down the broken pavement of Main Street, which, at its peak, had a dozen blocks of shops and businesses. Now the buildings were empty, some collapsing, some razed to sagebrush. In the desert, things decayed more slowly than they did in other places Randy had lived. The abandoned buildings had more charm here.

Randy turned down a street toward the old Post Office, a long, low structure with a solar-shingle roof and cinder-block sides.

The building had been converted to a ROA office. A sign out front (thirty years old—the newest thing in town) announced "Rural Outreach Administration — Lone Pine Field Office" with block letters in relief.

Randy hitched Blackeye to the sign, and went in.

RURAL
OUTREACH
ADMINISTRATION
LONE PINE BRANCH

Inside was dim compared to the cloudless midday sun he'd come from. Light spilled from the single front window into a waiting area, which opened into a room with four desks, only one of them occupied. Randy blinked and removed his hat. It smelled stale, a scent he associated with government.

"Mr. Leeworth?" the person behind the desk said, a small man with a black ponytail and a calm smile. Randy recognized him from the last visit, which was soon after he'd started seeing ghosts. He had thought, foolishly, the doctor might help with something like that.

"Yes," Randy said.

"Please have a seat. Dr. Lam will be out shortly. You can hang your hat on the rack." The man gestured to a coat rack in the corner.

"Thank you," Randy said, and did so. Not ten seconds later, a woman came in from a side door. He rose again as she approached.

"You must be Randy," she said, extending a hand to shake. "I'm doctor Lam."

"Pleased to meet you, doctor."

Her hand was warm and felt like easy confidence. She was a head and a half shorter than he, and two or three decades younger, but carried obvious authority. She had wide shoulders beneath her white lab coat, and a wide face with dark skin and attentive eyes.

"I see you've filled out the forms in advance."

"I did, yes."

"Great, come this way." Dr. Lam led Randy to an examination room and motioned for him to sit in one of the side chairs while she sat in the other. "So, what brings you in this month?"

"Well, the short of it is, doctor, my knee. It gets swollen and painful. Some days, it's hard to walk."

"Okay," said the doctor, writing a note on his chart with her tablet pen. "What kind of physical activity do you do, Randy? What's your normal day like?"

"Well, most days I like to hike to the top of the hill by my house. It's a 200-meter climb or so. There's a good path. Anyway, it's my favorite view."

"That's great. This is beautiful country, isn't it? It's only my second rotation up here."

Randy decided now that he liked this Dr. Lam. She was unguarded in the way of an honest person, and she cared about things outside herself. Both were more than he could say for the red-faced young doctor who saw him last time. That arrogant boy could not have been trusted with what Randy had to say.

"Welcome, doc. We're happy to have you."

She smiled. "What's the view of? The mountains? Or, I suppose you can see those from anywhere."

"True. But from Owl Ridge, you see the whole valley also. You look down over the town and the highway."

"I wouldn't think the highway was much to look at, from my sample of it."

"It is for me." Randy said.

Dr. Lam paused. "How is that?"

Now Randy paused. "I find the traffic interesting."

"Traffic? We didn't see another vehicle my entire way up here."

"Well, I can see cars on it most of the time."

"Cars?" The doctor looked perplexed.

"Well, ghost cars, if we're being honest." Randy was in deep now.

"Ghost cars?"

"Yes. Ghosts still like to use the highway, it seems. Sometimes I see them other places, walking, but mostly they drive on the highway."

The doctor gave him a hard look. "Do you mind if I run some general tests? It's been so long since you've been in for a checkup."

"As you like, doc."

Dr. Lam outfitted him with sensors, asked him to breathe and cough and look at a light. She ran blood and saliva and urine through analyzers. As she went, she explained the results of each test. She didn't run away with the detail, but she said it straight and didn't treat him like a fool. Randy was in the habit of judging people well and quickly, and it was his judgment that if Lam had been a chef, it would be a well-run kitchen.

In the end, Dr. Lam told Randy that she saw signs of inflammation, but otherwise he was in good health. Then she said, "So tell me more about these ghosts. How often do you see them?"

"Well, any time I go to the ridge, pretty much. So, every day. Sometimes I see them out on the land. Native ghosts, mainly, out there. And then if I come into town, like today."

"And do they look... ghostly? Or are they solid, like regular people? Can you tell the difference?"

"The ghosts are like flickers. I know they're there, but I don't see them exactly, except in flashes. If I try, I can kind of close my eyes to them altogether."

"Are you aware not everyone can see the ghosts?"

"Aware? Oh yes, I've never met anyone else who can. There was a man who lived in Ridgecrest who saw them, but I only heard about him."

"Why did you tell me? Weren't you afraid I wouldn't believe you?"

"You seemed like someone who appreciates the truth. And might know what to do with it." The doctor looked at him intensely. She was trying to judge him, he guessed, or decide something.

He wanted to say, 'Am I crazy, doc? Is it just chemistry? Can you give me a pill and make everything normal?' But, also, he didn't believe those things. He said nothing.

Dr. Lam's face softened and she inhaled. "We better take a closer look at that knee."

She brought out the multi-scanner, put a backing film behind the knee, and started up the machine.

"Are there any ghosts in here?" she asked, running a wand over the knee.

Randy shook his head. "Not today, doc."

"You've seen them before?"

"Last time I was here, a postman came through. He had the uniform, a satchel full of letters."

"You know this used to be a Post Office?"

"I've heard that, yes."

"Do the ghosts ever do anything, uh, scary?"

"I try not to cross paths with them up close. I don't think they can see me, most of the time, but I get a little chill. Every once in a while, one of them will want to pet my horse. That's when Blackeye gets spooked. I figure those are ghosts that used to ride. You can usually tell by the way they're dressed. Maybe they miss their horses."

"There aren't ghost horses? But there are ghost cars?"

"That's right, as far as I know."

"Have you always had these visions?"

"It's been a few years now that I can see the cars...." Randy's thoughts went to every quiet room, every empty alley, every time he flipped the lights off on the kitchen after a shift. That feeling. The native boy looking at him. How many times was it there? A hundred? A thousand? "But I reckon I've always noticed things other people don't."

Dr. Lam finished the scan. She looked up at Randy for a moment without saying anything. "I'm going to go take a look at the scan results. Would you wait here a few minutes?"

"As you like."

Dr. Lam left and closed the door. Before, only Lester knew the full story of the ghosts. Now there were two. Randy breathed in and tried to clear his head. Soon, Dr. Lam returned.

"So, I can see what's happening. It's basic tendinitis, very common. It's a minor problem now, but it will keep getting worse unless you fix it. I'm writing you a referral to see a specialist in Lancaster. She'll have several options for you. You should be able to get almost immediate relief."

"Lancaster? That's a lot to ask, doctor."

"I know it's far, but it's the closest equipped clinic."

"It's not the distance." Randy paused and the doctor gave him a questioning look. "I've lived in cities before. But that was before I... saw so much."

Dr. Lam looked at him for a moment, then turned to her tablet and began swiping. "You know, Mr. Leeworth, I grew up in Seattle."

"I lived there for a while," Randy said.

"Oh? So you may know, a long time ago, it was a city of tech barons."

"I've heard that, yes."

"People thought about the future all the time, and they made their fortunes on it." Randy waited for her to continue, "I wonder what it was like."

Randy watched her face draw into a melancholy smile as she looked up at him, "We live with so much of the past now. We all do."

"True enough."

"Whether you go is up to you. I'll give you something for the pain in the meantime."

Randy thanked the doctor, said his goodbyes, and left the itinerant office of the Rural Outreach Administration feeling unsure. He mounted Blackeye from the right side, forgetting that he'd been mounting from the left recently because of his knee. The move hurt.

He walked Blackeye up Main Street a few blocks then hitched her outside the general store. He filled the watering basin there from the tap, and went inside. Annette wasn't at the counter, but she would come out soon. Randy began filling tins and bags, getting groceries for Lester and himself. He did not want to go to Lancaster. He didn't want to see the source of that feeling in a motel room in a half-empty city.

Randy surveyed the case of synthetic meats. He did miss some of the foods he used to get in the Service Areas. But he was independent here. And peaceful. But then, there was Lester. No longer independent.

When he finished, Randy loaded up Blackeye and mounted. Before crossing Main Street, he stopped to look for ghost traffic. He saw none. But there was something else: a block up the street, a pair of ghosts walked toward him. He watched for a while, details flashing into view. It was a young couple. They shared an ice cream cone, playfully, and held hands. They were in love, perhaps. Randy smiled.

"So Blackeye, you up for a ride to Lancaster?"

TEAM SCUMM: MGMT.

ILLUSTRATIONS BY CLARE FULLER

SEAN CLANCY is *Planet Scumm's* esteemed editor-in-chief, meaning *he make word go right place* (but sometimes better).

Ensign Clancy also acts as the current Herald of Scummy, blessed to transcribe every errant whim of our intergalactic space deejay, praying all the while that the maniacal slime-bag achieves only half of his deranged fantasies.

This would normally be the line where Sean plugs some side project, but he's going to be shy instead and go for a meta joke that he'll later fail to justify to the rest of the team as "staying true to *Planet Scumm's* irreverent roots."

TYLER BERD herds cats for *Planet Scumm*. He acts as the ship's secretary, accountant, retail manager, and troubadour. Back on Earth, he works as a teacher and musician.

As managing editor, Ty keeps his third eye trained on the moving parts of the Scumm(TM) machinery. He prides himself on keeping the ship running only slightly behind schedule.

Planet Scumm's benevolent(?) overlord, Scummy, grew to sentience from a poorly monitored boil behind Ty's ear. And the rest, as they say, is history.

TEAM SCUMM: ART DEPT.

ILLUSTRATIONS BY CLARE FULLER

ALYSSA ALARCÓN SANTO puts her love of organization to use as *Planet Scumm*'s creative director. She lays out the books, pilots the illustration team, keeps the website rolling, and occasionally has time for some artwork.

Her time out-of-orbit is spent doing freelance illustration and design, often for literary or disability-centric projects.

She sometimes remembers to post on instagram @alyssasantodesign or, even less frequently, on twitter at @traitorlegs.

In this issue, Alyssa's art can be found:
» *Desert Man (photos harvested from Alyssa's mom's childhood), pg. 48*
» *Hector Brim, pg. 60*

SAM RHEAUME is *Planet Scumm*'s resident slush-reader, illustrator, and wild card marketer. When he's not contributing his multi-disciplinarian creative and editorial efforts to the zine, he spends his time working as the label czar at Jasper Hill Farm and/or corralling freelance writing and illustration contracts on the side.

Find him on instagram @sirheaume or call toll free at 1-800-GET-FUKD.

In this issue, Sam's art can be found:
» *Front cover*
» *Transmission Scumm, pg. VII*
» *Title page*
» *An Abridged History..., pg. 27*
» *The Door Man, pg. 37*

AUTHOR BIOS

JOE ANDERSON ("DESERT MAN") is an educator, fiction writer, and media studies scholar. His short story, "Parade", was published in *Johnny America*. *Strange Visitor: Subjectivity, Simulation, and the Future of the First Superhero*, an academic text, will be published by Lexington Books in 2021.

Bizarre thoughts about fiction can be found at his blog, *Dispatches from the Adventure*, available on YouTube and Wordpress.

JOACHIM HEIJNDERMANS (A LITTLE GALAXY) writes, draws, and paints nearly every waking hour.

Originally from the Netherlands, he's been all over the world, boring people by spouting random trivia about toys, movies and comics. His work has been featured in a number of anthologies and publications, such as *Mad Scientist Journal*, *Ahoy Comics*, and *The Gallery of Curiosities*. He's currently in the midst of completing his first children's book.

You can check out his other work at joachimheijndermans.com, or follow him on Twitter: @jheijndermans.

BEN HENNESY (AN ABRIDGED HISTORY OF THE END OF THE WORLD) is an author, playwright, and co-founder of the Chalkboard Theatre Project. His fiction has been published in *The Champagne Room*, *The Weird* and *Whatnot*, and his novelette *The Red Point Dilemma*, was a 2019 Gravity Award finalist.

When he isn't writing or teaching, he can often be found people-watching in the pubs or on the beaches of Dar es Salaam, Tanzania where he lives with his brilliant wife and the small pride of cats that have adopted them.

MATT HORNSBY (DEEP CLEAN) lives in Ireland. He has published work in *Metaphorosis*, *StarshipSofa* and *Electric Spec*, and is a graduate of the Odyssey writing workshop.

CHRISTOPHER MOYLAN (THE DOOR MAN) is an Associate Professor at NYIT and an activist in the areas of food security and social justice.

His work has appeared recently in *Parhelion*, *Fragmented Voices* and *Flea of the Dog*.

ASHLEY NAFTULE (A THOUSAND CRANES OF BLOOD AND STEEL) (they/them) is a writer & performer based in Phoenix, AZ.

A playwright and Associate Artistic Director at Space55 theatre, they've written and produced four plays: *Ear*, *The First Annual Bookburners Convention*, *The Canterbury Tarot*, and *Radio Free Europa*. A fifth play, *The Hidden Sea*, will premiere via YouTube in April 2021.

AUTHOR BIOS

They've previously been published in *Coffin Bell Journal, Bright Wall/Dark Room, and The AV Club.* They Tweet about movies, wrestling, and other miscellany as @ashleynaftule.

LAUREN O'DONOGHUE *(THESSALY)* is a writer and community organiser based in South Yorkshire, UK.

She graduated from Sheffield Hallam University with a first class honours degree in Creative Writing, and has most recently featured in the *Cranked Anvil Short Story Anthology.*

When she's not writing she enjoys watching folk horror movies, drinking malbec, and rabble rousing.

SAM REBELEIN *(HECTOR BRIM)* holds an MFA in Creative Writing from Goddard College.

His work has appeared in *Bourbon Penn, Shimmer, Ellen Datlow's Best Horror of the Year,* and elsewhere. He lives in Poughkeepsie, New York, and on Twitter @HillaryScruff.

STEFAN SOKOLOSKI *(KATU AND THE EYE OF FLESH)* is a massive weirdo, born and raised in the booger pits of the universe's left nostril. He also happens to be an author that writes stories steeped in the surreal. In his spare time he is a burger-flipping guru and a semi-decent Pikachu main in Smash Ultimate.

You can find occasional eccentric word blips over at @StefanSokoloski on twitter, and catch his story *"Being Under"* in TLDR Presses *Endless Pictures* collection.

JOSHUAH STOLAROFF *(GHOSTS OF LONE PINE)* is a writer, scientist, and musician living in Oakland, California, where he attempts to fight existential threats to humanity—or at least put them in jazzy pop songs.

His story collected in *Planet Scumm* is his first published work of fiction. This short story intersects with his upcoming novel, *Desert Crossing:* a science fiction western about a team navigating post-climate change California. He can be found at rationalcontemporary.com.

ILLUSTRATION TEAM

▼ **ERIKA SCHNATZ** is a doodler and designer who lives in Portland, Oregon, with her husband and the cutest (and least well-behaved) muppet-dog in the world. She's a Senior Production Artist at Image Comics where she gets to work on the layout and design of a whole bunch of comic books. In her free time she creates her own comics and illustrations. One of her annual projects is a tournament of cuteness called Cute K.O. Every March 16 characters go head-to-head until one cute creature remains. It's fun!

Erika's work is created with a mix of traditional and digital tools; she tends to do most drawing and linework with pencils and pens before scanning a piece to be cleaned up and/or colored in Photoshop. She's also recently become addicted to Posca paint pens and will not stop until she's collected them all (or has run out of expendable income).

In this issue, Erika's art can be found:
- » *Thessaly, pg. 1*
- » *A Little Galaxy, pg. 12*

MAURA "MOE" MCGONAGLE ▲ is a Boston-based illustrator, writer and editor carrying on the human tradition of storytelling. Best known for their vibrant figure work, Maura has created comics for several anthologies, including the upcoming *Starbound: A Space Sci-Fi Comics Anthology*. They specialize in narrative works and have created pieces for all ages, aiming to create dynamic, inclusive literature.

They can be found hanging out on twitter @doingartiguess or in the wild, probably lost.

In this issue, Moe's art can be found:
- » *Katu and the Eye of Flesh, pg. 48*
- » *Deep Clean, pg. 60*

CAMILLE VILLANUEVA is a jack-of-all-trades. Sometimes you'll find her puppeteering an 18 ft puppet, dressed up as Catwoman, or photographing formula one races. But given the times, you'll likely find her working from home, art directing and designing for Square. She lives in a converted ice-cream factory in Oakland with her partner and pup. In her spare time, she juggles a variety of personal projects: from writing music and gathering materials for her long list of cosplay dreams, to printmaking and playing Animal Crossing. Camille loves learning new things and she surrounds herself with plants and a growing collection of knick-knacks.

Camille is currently working on prints for her newly-opened online linoleum block print shop. Her prints are colorful and she enjoys layering blocks. Printmaking has always been a go-to medium. She loves how she gets lost in the carving and finds it very therapeutic. Camille has been documenting her process on Tiktok and Instagram. This year she's hoping to design more zines and fabric textiles.

▲ **CLARE FULLER** is an all-purpose creative type living her life in Salem. She is the editor-in-chief of *Saving Daylight*, a zine about seasonal sadness and the many ways we all deal with it. When she's not zine-ing, she works as a writer for a sustainable agriculture company, lurking in comic book shops, and hunting for the best bagel in Massachusetts.

In this issue, Clare's art can be found:
» *Team Scumm bios, pg. 141*

◄ You can find Camille's work at @camilleeeoo on Twitter, Instagram, and Tiktok. Her print shop is camilleeeoo.com.

In this issue, Camille's art can be found:
» *A Thousand Cranes of Blood and Steel, pg. 120*
» *Ghosts of Lone Pine, pg. 130*

PLANET SCUMM

THERE'S MORE SCUMM WHERE THAT CAME FROM, READER!

FIND OUR OTHER BOOKS AT PLANETSCUMM.SPACE

❑ **VOLUME 1:** *EVERYTHING! THE FIRST FOUR ISSUES*

❑ **ISSUE 5:** *HUMAN RESOURCES*

❑ **ISSUE 6:** *O SCUMM, ALL YE FAITHFUL*

❑ **ISSUE 7:** *A WRINKLE IN SLIME*

❑ **ISSUE 8:** *SIDEWAYS INFINITY*

❑ **ISSUE 9:** *A BLOODY PULP*

❑ **ISSUE 10:** *SUPERGIANT^x*

❑ **ISSUE 11:** *SNAKE EYES (COMING 2021)*

⧽ ALL BOOKS AVAILABLE AS PAPERBACKS AND EBOOKS ⧼
PICK UP AN ANNUAL SUBSCRIPTION FOR A FULL YEAR OF SCI-FI